## Dorsal fins cleaved the glassy surface

Half a dozen men charged onto the deck of the yacht. Their automatic rifles stabbed into the air and coughed an angry swarm at the Huey piloted by McCarter. He swung away in a violent arc, out of the range of fire.

The next salvo swept over the PT boat, and Encizo and Calvin James countered with a withering hail of lead from the starboard side until forced to duck for cover. Clad in wet suits, they were prepared to storm the yacht from the sea. They were casting apprehensive glances at the dark shapes gliding beneath the waters when they saw the gunship swoop toward the enemy yacht like a mechanical bird of prey.

Mack Bolan's

# PHOENIX FORCE®

# PHOENIX FORCE®

GAR WILSON

# KINGSTON CARNAGE

## A GOLD EAGLE BOOK FROM
# WORLDWIDE®

TORONTO • NEW YORK • LONDON • PARIS
AMSTERDAM • STOCKHOLM • HAMBURG
ATHENS • MILAN • TOKYO • SYDNEY

First edition May 1988

ISBN 0-373-61335-0

Special thanks and acknowledgment to
William Fieldhouse for his contribution to this work.

Printed in U.S.A.

## 1

The calypso band onstage was dressed in bright red suits and yellow shirts with frilly ruffles. The lead singer improvised words in a nursery-rhyme manner to the tune performed by the other band members. Guitar, flute and steel drum produced a complex combination of music, yet all blended together into a compelling beat.

The song was a pleasant bit of fluff about a man and a woman who find love on a remote island that is "pretty as can be in the Caribbean Sea." Perry and Teresa Hedge were delighted with the calypso music. The lyrics of the song hardly mattered to the young American couple, because everything about Jamaica was colorful and exciting to them.

Perry and Teresa were newlyweds, enjoying a honeymoon and dream vacation. Jamaica had a special appeal for the Hedges because Perry had proposed to Teresa during a commercial as they watched *The Deep* on television. The movie had become a sentimental favorite for the couple, who associated the romance and adventure of *The Deep* with the colorful setting of Jamaica in the film. They had decided it would be the ideal spot for an exciting vacation and a truly memorable honeymoon.

Jamaica didn't disappoint them. The Jamaican people seemed bright and friendly, eager to please the young tourists from Connecticut. Coconut-palm trees waved in the breeze as the Hedges gazed out the window of their hotel suite at the beaches. The swaying palms seemed to beckon to them to come forward and see the beautiful Caribbean in all its shimmering glory.

The Hedges went snorkeling off Port Royal. They were amazed by the great schools of tropical fish and small squid. The water was wonderful, as warm as that of a bathtub and as clear as freshly cleaned glass. They collected seashells and odd bits of coral, then lay on the golden beach and basked in the sun, sipping exotic drinks made with fruit juice and rum.

Most of the second day they spent strolling through the streets of Kingston, the capital city of Jamaica. They took a bus tour of St. John's Park and bought an assortment of curios and novelty items for gifts and mementos. Taken with what they saw, they snapped dozens of pictures, and had exhausted six rolls of film by evening.

The Blue Cuckoo, the popular restaurant they had chosen for their evening meal, featured reasonable prices, fine seafood and lots of atmosphere. The calypso band was a perfect complement to the tropical decor of the restaurant. Perry and Teresa were very much in love and happier than they had ever been.

A lot of customers in the Blue Cuckoo noticed the Hedges and later remarked how happy the couple seemed that night. They were good-looking and stood out in a crowd. Perry was six and a half feet tall, lean and athletic, with a rugged face framed by a blond mane of thick, wavy hair. Teresa was barely an inch over five feet, but her slender frame and proportionately long legs created an impression of greater height. Her jet-black hair and fine features revealed her Italian ancestry. More than one person had compared her dark, expressive eyes and full, sensuous lips to those of Sophia Loren.

The Hedges had finished their cocktails and were halfway through their shrimp salads when Perry complained about a pain in his stomach, and in a little while, Teresa began to utter half-choked cries of pain. The manager tried to calm the two Americans while a waiter called for an ambulance. By the time sirens wailed outside the Blue Cuckoo, most of the other customers had left the restaurant. Perry and Teresa had vomited on the floor before the manager could get them to his office. Their bodies were stiff and motionless when they were finally carried out on stretchers.

The ambulance pulled away from the Blue Cuckoo with sirens screaming and lights flashing. A police car suddenly appeared behind the ambulance and escorted it to the hospital, while another squad car came to a halt in front of the restaurant. The manager mopped his brow with a napkin as he apprehensively watched two uniformed figures emerge from the vehicle.

"I am police Sergeant Bristol, sir," a tall, formidable man with skin the color of black coffee announced as he filled the doorway. "Do you own this restaurant?"

"I'm one of the owners," the manager answered reluctantly. "I'm Carlton Fellows. Unfortunately, I was managing the place tonight."

"We got a report that two of your customers seem to have suffered food poisoning," Bristol remarked as he tucked his service cap under an arm and marched into the restaurant. "I assume that's why an ambulance just left from here."

The sergeant strolled into the dining area and glanced about at the empty chairs and vacant tables. The calypso band had been dismissed after the last of the customers departed, but the waiters, clerks and kitchen personnel were lined up like soldiers waiting for inspection. Everyone looked pretty uncomfortable, which was natural under the circumstances, Bristol realized. Nobody liked being questioned by the police, and he would have been somewhat suspicious of any bloke who seemed smug and confident in such a situation.

The restaurant employees were pretty much what he'd expected. The waiters, along with the cooks, were black, the cash-register clerk was a mulatto girl and the dishwashers were Asian mulattoes. Part Asian and part black, they were among the least favored of ethnic groups within Jamaica. Asian mulattoes were generally found in the lowest levels of employment.

The manager, Fellows, was a middle-aged white man, probably a British subject who had remained in Jamaica after the country had received full independence in 1962. Sergeant Bristol didn't like British Jamaicans. Although Bristol was too young to recall the time of the crown colony, he resented the British because they had formerly conducted the slave trade in Jamaica and had continued to govern Jamaica even after granting the country full autonomy in 1953.

Bristol glared at Fellows. The policeman secretly enjoyed his authority over the white man and wanted to see the restaurant owner squirm and sweat. It would be a pleasure to arrest Fellows for criminal negligence, Bristol thought, and if the American tourists had been poisoned by the Briton's food, the police sergeant would indeed get his wish.

"Nothing like this has ever happened before, Officer," Fellows began lamely. "We've always been very careful with food preparations. No one has ever gotten sick—"

"Until now," Bristol remarked dryly. "Did you throw out the food left on the Americans' plates? Don't suppose you'd want it sitting about, eh?"

"We didn't touch it, Sergeant," Fellows answered. "We assumed you'd want it for evidence. That's their food over there on that table."

"It is?" Bristol turned toward the table. He frowned slightly, almost disappointed that Fellows hadn't tossed out the food and couldn't be accused of trying to cover up some heinous error. "Well, we'll have it analyzed. What about the rest of your customers? None of them complained of illness to-night?"

"No," Fellows assured him. "None of the other customers were ill, and many of them also had the shrimp salad tonight. Of course, I had my waiters get their names and addresses in case any suffer from ill effects after returning home."

"You'd better hope and pray those Americans recover and no one else falls ill from your tainted food, Mr. Fellows," Bristol warned. "And I advise you not to think about leaving the country for a while. Not until this matter is cleared up. I also suggest you contact your lawyers. You'll probably need them before this is over."

"Excuse me, Officer," one of the cooks began as he stepped forward. "I believe you ought to know about somethin' we found in my kitchen tonight."

"Oh?" Bristol smiled, eager to learn their discovery. "Something with the food, sir?"

"No," the cook replied as he turned toward a table to point at an object bundled in a soiled apron. "This has nothin' to do with my cookin', mon. It's somethin' I don't wants to even look at again if I don't has to, Officer."

Sergeant Bristol grunted and walked to the table. He unfolded the cloth and pulled back the apron to uncover two crudely made dolls. One, a masculine figure, wore a white shirt or jacket across the stiff cloth arms projecting from its stick skeleton. Yellow straw extended from the back of the doll's clay head, and two blue buttons had been stuck in place for eyes.

The other doll was clad in a poorly sewn yellow dress. Coarse black hair hung from the feminine figure's clay skull, and dark stones had been placed in the doll's face for eyes. Both dolls had long hat pins thrust through their bellies and thorns driven into the clay between their symbolic eyes.

"What sort of nonsense is this?" Bristol demanded, turning on the restaurant staff with fire in his eyes and fury in his voice. "Did Fellows or this cook come up with this farce?"

"I object to that accusation, Sergeant," Fellows said sharply. "None of us had an opportunity to make those nasty little figurines. At least, none of us could have done it *after* the couple became ill."

"You're saying these damn dolls were in the kitchen *before* the Americans sat down to supper?" Bristol frowned. He glanced down at the figures. "Did anyone notice if they were dressed in a manner similar to these dolls?"

"The man wore a white shirt and the woman a yellow summer dress," Fellows confirmed. "He was a blonde and she had black hair. I'd say it's likely whoever planted those dolls in the kitchen had those Americans in mind."

Bristol glared at the manager and his employees in amazement. "You're saying this was attempted murder?"

"It's worse than murder, Mr. Sergeant," the cook declared grimly. "You know what this is as sure as I do, mon. Somebody put a juju on them folks."

"Rubbish," Bristol scoffed, yet he felt a cold ball of fear form in his belly as he glanced once more at the figurines. "Voodoo dolls and witchcraft. It's all nonsense, and you know it."

"I ain't gonna say what is and what isn't when it comes to things I don't understand," the cook replied. "But I knows enough not to laugh at a juju, and I knows devil's work when I sees it."

Bristol wrapped the dolls in the apron and muttered something under his breath. The figurines were evidence, despite the seemingly ridiculous supposition of witchcraft and magic. He handed the bundle to the other policeman and instructed him to lock the dolls in the trunk of the patrol car until further notice. Just then the telephone rang, and Fellows answered it.

"It's for you, Sergeant Bristol," the manager announced, offering the telephone receiver to the officer. "A Lieutenant Smith wishes to speak to you."

"Thank you," the sergeant said, taking the phone and speaking into the mouthpiece. "Bristol here." He listened solemnly and said he understood before he hung up and turned to Fellows.

"Lieutenant Smith is a homicide investigator," Bristol explained, his manner even more grave than before. "He called from the hospital. The two young Americans both died less than ten minutes ago. Smith will be here as soon as possible to begin looking into this matter personally."

"So it is murder," Fellows said, shaking his head.

"Devil's work," Bristol corrected. He didn't smile when he said it.

## 2

"Eleven Americans dead," Hal Brognola announced as he tossed a bundle of file folders on the conference table. "None of them were politicians, espionage agents, wealthy businessmen or celebrities of any kind. Every one of them was just a plain ordinary tourist, and the only thing they all had in common is that they were on vacation in Jamaica when they got killed."

"I take it we're not talking about a tour bus that had a fatal crash near Kingston," David McCarter remarked, a trace of impatience slipping into his voice.

"We're talking about murder," Brognola replied grimly. "Cold-blooded, systematic murder."

"The victims are just tourists?" Yakov Katzenelenbogen inquired, thoughtfully drumming the steel hooks of the prosthesis at the end of his right arm against the tabletop. "You're sure these people aren't connected with any intelligence organizations or involved in any sort of radical politics?"

"Aaron cross-checked every individual's name through his computers," Brognola answered, striking a wooden match against a stone paperweight as though he were testing it. He let the flame go out while he clenched a fat cigar between his teeth. "The Bear didn't find anything even vaguely suspicious about the backgrounds of any of the victims."

The five men seated around the table in front of Brognola nodded solemnly. "The Bear" was Aaron Kurtzman, the resident computer wizard of Stony Man operations. His computers could tap the data centers of every major intelligence organization, all five branches of the U.S. military and the police departments of more than three hundred major cities. Kurtzman could plug into information banks of the IRS, the Pentagon or Interpol. If the Bear said the Americans murdered in Jamaica had nothing suspicious in their backgrounds, then they must have had histories that read like bit parts in a Disney film.

Kurtzman had been confined to a wheelchair after receiving a bullet in the spine when enemies had launched an assault on Stony Man headquarters. Yet the Bear was still the best computer jockey in the business. The Stony Man crew consisted of only the best people in the fields of expertise needed for the supersecret organization.

Unlike most clandestine outfits, Stony Man was less concerned with gathering intelligence than with taking direct action against special targets. It was a small elite unit commanded by Hal Brognola. The Fed took orders only from the President of the United States. No one else in the federal government even knew Stony Man existed.

Brognola was chief of operations for Stony Man and gave assignments to the special commando teams that were the enforcement arm of the organization.

The five men seated at the conference table in the Stony Man War Room comprised Phoenix Force, the most unique and highly professional elite strike force ever created.

Yakov Katzenelenbogen was the unit commander. A middle-aged Israeli colonel who had formerly been a resistance fighter against the Nazis in Europe during the Second World War, Katz's combat experience since then had been remarkable. He had been a guerrilla warrior for the independence of the state of Israel and a battlefield commander during the Six-Day War and in dozens of lesser-known conflicts. He had also served with Mossad, Israel's primary intelligence network, and had worked with most of the major spy outfits of the United States and Western Europe, including the American CIA, the British SIS and the West German BND. Katz was one of the most experienced and highly skilled espionage operatives in history.

David McCarter was an ex-SAS sergeant who had seen action as a "special observer" in Vietnam, in the battle-scarred hills of Oman and on the streets of Northern Ireland. The bold Briton had participated in Operation Nimrod, the spectacular SAS raid on the Iranian Embassy in London in 1980, and he'd been part of a covert "police action" in Hong Kong the following year. The tall, fox-faced Briton was an ace pilot, a champion pistol marksman and an expert in virtually every form of warfare.

Rafael Encizo had been born and raised in Havana, Cuba. His family had been scooped up by Castro's soldiers after the Communist takeover. Most of his loved ones had been executed. His younger brother and two sisters were taken to a "reeducation center," and only young Rafael escaped. But he returned to Cuba with the Bay of Pigs invasion force and was captured and held prisoner in El Principe, where he endured near-starvation, beatings and torture without breaking. One day a guard got careless with Encizo. The prisoner broke the jailer's neck and successfully escaped from the political prison. Then he returned to the United States, where he worked as a professional bodyguard, scuba instructor, treasure hunter and insurance investigator before Stony Man enlisted him for Phoenix Force.

Gary Manning was a big man, built like a Canadian lumberjack. Indeed, Manning was Canadian and an accomplished woodsman and hunter. He was also one of the best demolitions experts in the world. Manning had used his skills with a rifle and explosives as an "observer" in Vietnam attached to the 5th Special Forces. He later worked with the West German GSG-9 antiterrorist squad in the 1970s. A human workhorse with an incredible amount of physical and mental endurance, Manning turned to the world of business and soon became chief security adviser and executive vice president of a major North American import-export business. Manning had been on his way to the top when he accepted an invitation to join Phoenix Force.

Calvin James had been drafted into Phoenix Force for a mission that required a man who was both a skilled warrior and an expert chemist. A tall, athletic black who had been raised in a hellhole ghetto on the south side of Chicago, James joined the Navy at the age of seventeen and became a hospital corpsman with the elite Sea, Air and Land team. He served with the SEALs in Vietnam and later attended UCLA on the GI bill to pursue a career in medicine and chemistry.

The tragic and violent deaths of his sister and mother steered James into a major change in career. He turned to law enforcement and joined the San Francisco Police Department. James was a member of a SWAT team when Phoenix Force virtually kidnapped him to try to enlist his aid for a mission. They accomplished the assignment, but Keio Ohara, the original fifth member of Phoenix Force, was killed in action. Calvin James was the natural choice to replace the slain warrior, and he had willingly stayed with Phoenix Force ever since.

"Do they have any idea why these tourists were killed?" James inquired, glancing through a file folder. "You know, something nice and simple like robbery, maybe?"

"If this was just a rash of ruthless thieves who didn't care if they killed people in the process, I wouldn't have called you guys to this meeting," Brognola answered, biting down on his cigar as if trying to demolish it. "We can't send Phoenix Force to handle every crime wave that occurs in this hemisphere, even if American citizens are the victims. Whatever motive the killers might have for murdering American citizens in Jamaica, robbery isn't it. Not a single victim was robbed, according to these reports."

"Well, Jamaica has seen its share of political tension and violence," Encizo commented, leaning back in his seat. "Any terrorists or extremists taking credit for these murders?"

"None," the Fed answered, "and there hasn't been any escalation of anti-American or pro-Marxist activity, either. The police are puzzled by the killings, and they don't really have any idea where to start. There seems to be only one clue that keeps popping up with each murder. Every one of them is somehow linked to voodoo."

"Voodoo?" McCarter scoffed. "If I didn't know better, I'd figure this was some sort of elaborate practical joke."

"Nobody's laughing, David," Brognola said grimly. "The prime minister of Jamaica isn't laughing, and neither is the President. The families of the murder victims sure don't think it's funny."

"I didn't mean anything of that sort," the Briton said with a shrug. "It's just that stories about bloody voodoo are the sort of thing you expect to hear around a campfire in the middle of the night. Never thought we'd get a mission to go hunt down some blokes who've been stickin' pins in dolls."

"That's what we're doing, David," Manning declared. He had discovered a photograph of the two figurines that had been found at the Blue Cuckoo after Perry and Teresa Hedge had fallen ill. "Take a look at this."

"Read the file," Brognola urged. "You'll see that there was nothing supernatural about the deaths of those young people. They were poisoned. Food was laced with belladonna."

"Belladonna?" James raised his eyebrows. "That's interesting. It's a natural poison found in plants of the *Solanaceae* family. Doesn't require a chemist to use belladonna for a poison. Used to be pretty popular among poisoners way back during the Roman Empire and the Middle Ages. Supposedly you can't smell it or taste it, but it leaves a red rash on the skin of the victim."

"You must have covered some weird subjects in chemistry classes back in California," Encizo commented.

"Herbal medicines were the original form of chemistry," James explained with a thin smile. "So were herbal poisons. Whoever the killers are, they must favor old-fashioned formulas over synthetic poisons."

"You said eleven Americans were killed," Katz began thoughtfully, flicking his Ronson lighter to fire up a Camel cigarette. "Were they all poisoned, Hal?"

"Most of them," Brognola answered. "A pair of senior citizens, who'd saved up for God knows how long to take a nice sunny vacation in the Caribbean, were found dead in their hotel room. They'd both been decapitated."

"Yeah," Encizo said, examining the grisly photos in one of the file folders. "I've got that case here. Ethel and Dennis Jackson. Their naked bodies were found in the bathroom, slumped next to the tub, their hands were tied behind their backs with lamp cords. Must have been a goddamn nightmare for an elderly couple like that.''

''Doesn't sound like it would be a lot of fun for anybody at any age,'' James commented dryly. ''Were the severed heads missing?''

''No,'' Encizo answered, consulting the file. ''The maid found the heads when she entered the room to make the bed. The heads were sitting on the pillows on the bed. Poor woman probably screamed her head off, but maybe that's not the best expression to use under the circumstances.''

''*Cristo,*'' the Cuban muttered, his face screwing up with disgust. ''The mouths had been stuffed with salt and the lips sewed shut.''

''That's sick,'' Manning said, shaking his head. ''What kind of lunatic would do something like that?''

''That sounds vaguely familiar,'' Katz remarked, blowing a smoke ring across the table. ''Salt was once regarded as a substance for purification—still is among some cultures. Believed to drive off evil spirits or something like that. During the witchcraft trials of the Spanish inquisition, witches were decapitated and their mouths were stuffed with salt to keep the devil from bringing them back to life.''

''Similar legends are found in voodoo folklore,'' James added. ''People have a tendency to associate voodoo with the old animistic religions of Africa, but it actually borrowed as much from Christianity as from any other source.''

"I'd forgotten you know a bit about this hocus-pocus hogwash," McCarter commented. "In fact, that came up in your first mission with us, the time we took on those blokes from Haiti who called themselves the Black Alchemists."

"Yeah," James replied. "And I told you then that followers of voodoo consider it to be a religion. They don't think it's bullshit."

"Okay," Manning said, trying to prevent an argument. "Why would voodoo practitioners chop off somebody's head and stuff the mouth with salt?"

"To prevent the dead from coming back as a zombie," James explained. "You know, like in *Night of the Living Dead*?"

"Sounds pretty crazy," Encizo remarked, "but I think Calvin's right. A form of voodoo called obeah has been practiced in Jamaica for hundreds of years. Maybe the followers of some fanatic cult of voodoo or obeah have decided to kill off Americans for some reason we can't even guess. Apparently the Jamaican cops can't figure it out either."

"The President thinks this is serious enough to send Phoenix Force to take care of it," Brognola announced. "Americans getting murdered is bad enough under any circumstances, but what's happening in Jamaica is practically genocide of U.S. tourists. Some of the President's advisers think Communists from Cuba or Nicaragua may be responsible. The Jamaicans are also upset. Tourism is a vital industry there. The economy suffered terribly after the riots and street violence in '84 and '85 scared away a lot of tourists.

Jamaica seemed to have pretty well recovered from that setback, and now this happens.''

"When the economy goes to hell, the government in power is apt to fall from grace," Katz remarked. "Perhaps even fall from power."

"Indeed," Brognola confirmed. "The United States doesn't want to see the present administration in Jamaica lose power. The former prime minister was a socialist who admired Fidel Castro and was slowly grooming his nation toward either a Communist system or a form of socialism very sympathetic to the Communists. I don't have to remind any of you what country is right next door to Jamaica."

"You mean Cuba?" Encizo inquired. "Maybe we ought to consider another neighbor of Jamaica's—Haiti. The voodoo connection seems more the style of Haitians than Cubans. Of course, it could just be that the more radical obeah cults are acting up, but I can't begin to guess what they hope to accomplish."

"You guys get the job," Brognola declared. "You unravel the mysteries after you get there and take care of the problem. Nobody does that better than Phoenix Force. Gary, you sure you're fit for duty?"

"My arm had three months to heal," Manning assured him. "I'm quite ready for field duty now."

"Good," the Fed said with a nod. "We'll fly you there via a Navy chopper from an aircraft carrier on maneuvers in the area. That way we don't have to worry about customs and crap like that. Transporting weapons and other equipment won't be a problem. The governor-general himself will sign the special weapons permits you'll need while in Jamaica. Can you be ready by morning?"

"We can be ready in two hours, Hal," Katz answered.

"You'll leave in the morning," Brognola insisted. "I suggest you enjoy the few hours you've got until then. Don't expect to find a Caribbean paradise when you get to Jamaica."

**3**

He called himself Cercueil, but that wasn't his real name. He had adopted the name three years previously after learning of the death of the original Cercueil. He had also changed his manner of dress and personal behavior. The transformation had occurred when the spirit of Maurice Cercueil came to him one night. Their souls had joined, and Maurice Cercueil had chosen his successor to continue his name and carry out his ambitions.

Or so Cercueil—the "new" Cercueil—claimed.

Not everyone believed that of course. Many realized it was simply a theatrical trick to impress the more gullible and superstitious members among them. Yet none could fault the results of the tactic. The new Cercueil played his role well. He always wore a formal black suit with a black tie and a matching silk top hat. The outfit would have seemed absurd unless one realized the black top hat was reminiscent of Baron Samedi, the lord of the legions of the dead in voodoo folklore.

He carried a black swagger stick with a silver skull handle, identical to the sinister scepter carried by the original Cercueil. He never removed his dark glasses, not even when indoors or at night. The new Cercueil played his role as skillfully as his namesake had before him.

The first Cercueil had been a showman. The head of the infamous Ton Ton Macoute during the rule of François "Papa Doc" Duvalier, Maurice Cercueil had adopted his strange costume to play on the beliefs and fears of Haitians who believed in voodoo. Even the name "Cercueil" had probably been a prop. It was unlikely that the head of the Ton Ton Macoute had really been born with the family name "Coffin."

The new Cercueil had formerly been known as Pierre Mazarin. Mazarin had been a captain in the Ton Ton Macoute under Jean-Claude Duvalier, the son of Papa Doc. One of the most feared and hated secret police organizations in history, the Ton Ton Macoute had been named after the demon-thieves of voodoo legend, which prowled the night and abducted children. Captain Mazarin had learned the value of terror when he'd served with the Ton Ton Macoute. Fear could be as effective as violence in subduing the rebellious masses. In Haiti, nothing was more feared than the dark side of voodoo.

Realizing that, Papa Doc had encouraged the rumors of his alleged supernatural powers among the largely illiterate and superstitious Haitians. The senior Duvalier had ruled until his death in 1971 and had been succeeded by "Baby Doc," who was to be less successful than his father.

Captain Mazarin believed that he knew why Jean-Claude Duvalier had failed to remain in power. In

Mazarin's opinion, Baby Doc did not understand the Haitian people. The young dictator lacked his father's understanding of the power of voodoo over the island nation. Baby Doc had attempted to make reforms—at least publicly—to improve Haiti's image in the rest of the world. But when political opponents and union leaders had made problems, Baby Doc ordered the Ton Ton Macoute to crack down on them with mass arrests and brute force.

Perhaps, Mazarin suspected, if Jean-Claude Duvalier had kept Maurice Cercueil as head of the Ton Ton Macoute, he might still be in power. Cercueil had understood the fears of the Haitian people. The fears of shadows that breathed and eyes that saw through the faces of pagan gods. Cercueil had started rumors that he was a *bocor*, a sorcerer who could kill with a curse and raise the dead to do his bidding. The Haitian peasants had been terrified of Cercueil.

Baby Doc had been scared of the Ton Ton Macoute, as well, and had forced Cercueil into exile. The "Coffin" had fled to the United States and created a crime network that attempted to blackmail the federal government into financing his return to Haiti and his planned overthrow of Jean-Claude. The scheme went sour, and Maurice Cercueil was eventually hunted down by Phoenix Force and killed in a battle at his mountain fortress in Colorado.

Jean-Claude Duvalier's schemes did not fare much better. Riots and demonstrations in Haiti had increased, and even the Ton Ton Macoute could not control the outraged masses. In January, 1986, fearful that Baby Doc's regime was about to fall, Captain Mazarin and many of his comrades fled Haiti. In February, the Duvalier regime collapsed, and the dictator and his family fled to France.

Mazarin and his Ton Ton Macoute had come to roost in Jamaica. They kept a low profile, fearful of being deported back to Haiti. That fate was indeed terrifying to consider. Many former members of the Duvalier secret police had been killed in the streets by mobs of angry Haitians who finally had an opportunity to strike back at the vicious storm troopers who had terrorized them for almost three decades.

In Jamaica, the Ton Ton Macoute renegades gradually formed a plan to allow them to seize power and authority once again. Mazarin's transformation into Cercueil had been part of the scheme. The new Cercueil's dreams of conquest were actually more ambitious than his namesake's, and the risks seemed to be far less.

The man who had come to be known as Pierre Mazarin Cercueil sat behind a large mahogany desk in the air-conditioned cabin of his floating headquarters. His tall, lean frame rested comfortably in the leather armchair as he peered at the two men who stood on the opposite side of the desk. His long ebony fingers stroked the black shaft of the swagger stick on the desk top as he listened to Louis de Broglie's report on the progress of the Ton Ton Macoute operations in Jamaica.

"Everything seems to be going quite smoothly," de Broglie declared. "The United States is warning

Americans not to travel to Jamaica because the risk to tourists is too great. The authorities suspect pro-Marxist terrorists as being responsible for the deaths. The police suspect members of a local obeah cult killed the tourists. The People's National Party is accusing the administration and the Jamaican Labour Party of incompetence. The JLP is likewise accusing the PNP of helping to stir up trouble and supporting Communist factions they believe to be behind the killings."

Cercueil smiled as he raised a cup of rum-laced tea to his lips. "Everyone is looking in the wrong direction. The fools will soon be fighting among themselves so fiercely they won't even realize their country is slipping away from them."

Louis de Broglie nodded. He was a big man with broad shoulders, a chest as big as a keg of nails and hands that could easily have served as shovels. In Haiti, the muscular Ton Ton Macoute thug had enjoyed crushing the skulls of peasants with his bare hands.

Yet de Broglie was not a dumb brute. Within his powerful body was a shrewd mind. Cercueil was too clever to choose a second-in-command just because the guy was big or well muscled. Louis de Broglie was a good organizer, well respected by both the other Ton Ton Macoute and the Jamaican underworld hoodlums connected with the conspiracy. He was also loyal to Cercueil. De Broglie was the only man Cercueil could truly trust, the only person he could consider his friend.

"You're jumpin' to a lot of conclusions awful quick, my Haitian friend," Montgomery Penn declared as he reached inside his white silk jacket for a pack of Turkish cigarettes. "So a few American tourists are dead. You think that means you can take over an entire country? Mon, you'd better put your feet back on firm ground before you float away on inflated egos."

Louis de Broglie glared at the Jamaican gangster. Penn was a mulatto, his skin a lighter shade than many a white with a deep tan. He smiled often, a mocking grin that displayed two gold teeth. Penn liked gold. His Rolex, rings, necklaces and cigarette holder were all made of gold. De Broglie considered him a flashy, arrogant petty crook who had probably risen to the top of the criminal sewer in Kingston by sheer luck rather than ability.

Cercueil knew better. Penn might dress like a pimp, but he was no fool. The Jamaican did not give a damn if the Haitians liked him or not, and he did not care if he offended them. Penn was smart enough to realize they would not kill him as long as they needed him. Right now, they needed him. When that changed, Penn planned to take his blood money from Cercueil and head for the Bahamas.

"You have a good point, Mr. Penn," Cercueil said, keeping his voice soft and even as he nodded approval of Penn's observation. "But we're judging success by what has happened thus far, and everything has gone exactly as planned. I'll admit that blind optimism is a weakness and overconfidence can be a fatal sin. Still, we must believe in what we're doing if we're going to accomplish our goals.''

"Taking over Jamaica is gonna be quite a feat, mon," Penn remarked. "I don't even understand why you want to do this, let alone understand everythin' about how you plan to accomplish it."

"Those aren't your concerns, Mr. Penn," Cercueil said politely. "I don't think you'll understand this, but I'm doing all this because I'm a patriot."

"A patriot?" Penn laughed. "I never thought of the Ton Ton Macoute as patriots—"

"Who do you think held Haiti together since 1957?" Cercueil demanded, a trace of outrage in his tone. "Who do you think served the interests of President Duvalier, enforced his laws and crushed his enemies? Who do you think maintained order and kept the whole nation from slipping into chaos?"

"Never thought of it that way before," Penn confessed, keeping his true thoughts to himself, wisely avoiding a political debate with the powerful voodooist.

"For fourteen years we kept the scum in their place and protected our president," Cercueil continued. "Then Duvalier died and that spoiled brat son of his took over. They called him 'Baby Doc,' and that's what he was. A squawking, ignorant baby who'd been raised on a satin pillow. He wanted world approval, and actually considered disbanding the Ton Ton Macoute to try to get it. Officially, that is; actually, we were still carrying on business as usual. Baby Doc was ashamed of us and wanted to pretend we weren't there.

He should have listened to us but he didn't, and he lost power because of it.

"I know most people think it's wonderful that Jean-Claude fled Haiti," Cercueil said with a sneer. "In fact, he wasn't half the ruler his father was. But look, what has happened to Haiti since? There is no real government in Haiti. Not one in five Haitians can read or write. How are they supposed to govern themselves? They're like superstitious children who need a strong father to keep them in line. I'm going to give them that—and a lot more as well."

"You intend to give Jamaica to Haiti?" Penn was stunned by the notion. He began to wonder if Cercueil was really insane.

"I intend to unite the two countries under a single strong government," the Ton Ton Macoute boss declared. "Haiti has nothing but coffee and sugar and mangoes. Mining operations are poorly handled and use outdated equipment. Manufacturing is crude and backward. That will change when I can share the technology of Jamaica with my homeland. Haiti will become strong when aided by the modern mining, processing and agricultural techniques of this country. After I seize control of Jamaica, Haitians will beg me to save them, too. They will beg the Ton Ton Macoute to return order and discipline to our nation."

"I see," Penn lied, thinking that was probably what Cercueil wanted to hear. "But why kill these American tourists? Why all this voodoo crap, mon?"

"There's more than one reason, Mr. Penn," Cercueil assured him with a broad smile. "It all has to do with turning Jamaica into chaos. Unfortunately for the Americans, they happen to be the most important part of Jamaica's tourist trade. Twenty years ago, we'd have been killing Britons instead. Actually, the plan probably wouldn't work if Jamaica was still a British dependency. Look what happened in the Falkland Islands.''

"You really think you can get away with this?'' Penn asked, regretting the question as soon as it slipped out.

"Absolutely,'' Cercueil laughed as he rapped the silver skull handle of his swagger stick on the desk. "We've got the power of voodoo behind us. You know something, Mr. Penn? Before we're finished, a lot of people who never believed in voodoo before will have suddenly gained a new respect and fear of our unique religion. Maybe even you will become a true believer after you see what we're going to do in the next phase of our mission.''

"I guess it's possible,'' Penn answered with a wooden nod. He no longer had any doubt about Cercueil's sanity.

**4**

The man's scream filled the fifth-floor corridors of the Sir Alexander Hotel. Few guests dared to open their doors to see the source of the terrible cry, and no one who heard it would forget the sound soon. The scream seemed to express the utmost fear and horror that any human being could experience.

Those who actually peered from their rooms saw a grisly scene that could have occurred in a nightmare. Indeed, the witnesses would probably be haunted by recurring images of the terrible sight in their dreams.

A middle-aged white man, dressed in a white shirt and gray slacks, lay sprawled across the carpet. His skull was split open; blood and brains oozed from his wrecked head. Next to the corpse stood an emaciated figure, a bloodstained machete clenched in his bony black hands. The scrawny assassin was dressed in ragged clothes caked with dirt. Tiny white maggots crawled across his filthy torn shirt.

The human scarecrow moaned and uttered strange grunting sounds as he gazed down at the dead man, seemingly barely aware of what he was looking at. His eyes rolled upward, the bloodshot whites a stark contrast to the dark, dirt-smeared, skeletal face. Staggering away from the dead man, the loathsome figure walked unsteadily through the corridor, grasping the machete in a frozen two-handed grip.

Not surprisingly, none of the guests ventured from their rooms. Most were too frightened to do anything but lock their doors and pray. One vomited on the carpet; two others had enough sense to call the front desk and report the homicide.

An unsuspecting maid, humming a popular calypso melody, emerged from the elevator and pushed her cart of towels and bed sheets into the hallway, then around the corner. She screamed, seeing the terrible figure with the bloodied jungle knife, and stepped back as the killer raised his weapon. From the assassin's mouth came a bestial bellow, and his eyes were wide with irrational fury.

The maid turned to run. The sharp edge of the machete chopped into the back of her skull. It cleaved bone and sank deep into her brain. Her scream was abruptly terminated. The killer yanked the blade free and shuffled down the corridor.

"Oh, my God!" a hotel security guard gasped as he opened the door to the stairwell at the fifth floor.

The guard saw the two bodies and the monstrous killer, who was staggering around the hall like a dazed and disoriented beast. He was quick to sum up the situation. But the guard did not carry a gun, and he was not about to take on a maniac with a machete armed only with his nightstick. So he ducked into the stairwell and bolted down to the lobby.

"Call the police!" he cried. "For the love of God, hurry!"

"What is it?" the desk clerk asked as the guard galloped into the lobby, nearly colliding with a party of guests about to sign the register. "What did you find up there?"

"It..." the guard began, gasping for breath. "It's a...a zombie...."

PHOENIX FORCE ARRIVED at Kingston International Airport to find Colonel Jonathan J. Wells waiting for them. A portly black man with a ready smile and wire-rimmed glasses with thick lenses, the top intelligence officer of the governor-general's council on internal security cheerfully greeted the five new arrivals, waved aside the customs inspectors, and escorted them to the black-and-green tour bus parked outside the airport.

"I'm certainly glad you chaps made it," Wells declared, his accent revealing Britain's long influence in Jamaica. "There's been talk about the cancellation of flights coming from the U.S. until this dreadful business is settled. Of course, you came in on a Navy copter, so I don't suppose that would have affected you much, anyway. Still, glad you landed here so I could meet you personally."

"We appreciate that, Colonel," Yakov Katzen-elenbogen assured him, loading his luggage into the rear of the bus. "Although we did want to keep a low profile."

"I know, I know," Wells replied with a deep sigh. "But the governor-general wanted you to come di-

"I know, I know," Wells replied with a deep sigh. "But the governor-general wanted you to come directly to Kingston because this is where most of the trouble seems to be happening. Wants us all to get on it immediately. He can't wait to get everything cleared up, because this awful business is causing all sorts of nasty problems."

"Those folks who got murdered probably thought it was pretty nasty, too," Gary Manning said dryly, selecting a seat inside the tour bus.

"If the victims hadn't been white, I doubt your government would have sent you here," the driver muttered sourly.

"Ethel and Dennis Jackson were an elderly black couple from Detroit," Calvin James retorted. "They got their heads cut off while on vacation here. Does that make you feel any better, man?"

"I didn't know about the Jacksons," the driver said with a shrug.

"Oh, this is Sergeant Bristol of the Kingston police," Colonel Wells said, introducing the driver to Phoenix Force. "He was involved in a couple of the investigations in the city."

"Obviously the Jackson homicides weren't among them," James commented.

"That's right," Bristol offered. "You Americans never make mistakes, so I'm sure you'll solve this matter in a day or two. If not, you'll find a way to blame your failure on us Jamaicans."

"That's uncalled-for, Sergeant," Wells told him.

"Don't worry about it, Colonel," Rafael Encizo assured Wells. "We'll just ignore the sergeant until he has something to say that's worth listening to."

"What about the fact that another American was murdered at the Sir Alexander Hotel less than an hour ago?" Bristol asked with a coy smile. "Heard it on the police radio while you fellows were busy at the airport."

"That's bloody cute," David McCarter snapped. "How long did you plan to sit on that information, mate? Or did you just make it up to get us pissed off?"

"If you're calling me a liar—" Bristol began, his eyes narrowing with anger.

"Nobody's calling you anything yet," Katz declared. "What details did you hear concerning the murder?"

"A white male with an American passport and a maid working at the hotel were both killed by a lunatic with a machete," Bristol replied. "Police were called in and shot the killer when he came at them with the knife. Apparently he's dead, too. Guess you'll have to give credit to the Kingston police, after all. Correct?"

"We don't have anything against the Kingston police except that they've got you on the force," James answered. He grinned when Bristol glared at him.

"Can we go straight to the police headquarters?" Katz asked, turning to Colonel Wells. "We'd like to get all the information possible as fast as we can. You'll convince the police to cooperate with us, Colonel?"

"That shouldn't be a problem," Wells confirmed.

"You might use your pull with the medical examiner, too," James added. "I want to participate in the autopsies of the two latest victims, and especially the autopsy of the dude the cops wasted."

"You're a doctor?" Bristol asked, surprised.

"No, but I watch *St. Elsewhere* every week," James replied. "Reruns of *Quincy*, too. Handling a couple autopsies will be a breeze, man."

"Just a minute," Katz warned. "There's no sense in all of us going to the police yet. We don't have enough information to put too much trust in the police."

"What's that supposed to mean?" Bristol demanded.

"It means there are crooked cops everywhere," Encizo replied. "There's always a possibility one of your fellow police officers is secretly working with the people we're trying to hunt down. Nothing against you or the Kingston police. But we just can't afford to take chances."

"So you don't trust us, either?" Bristol asked, tilting his head toward Colonel Wells.

"We trust you to a degree," Encizo said with a shrug. "If that's not good enough for you, then you'll just have to be patient until we decide we can trust you a bit more."

"Mr. Johnson and I will see the police," Katz stated, using Calvin James's cover name. "The rest of you can take a cab—make that two cabs to haul all the luggage—and head for the Royal Hamlet Hotel. Secure rooms for all of us, and Johnson and I will meet you there later."

"You need anything from your gear?" McCarter inquired as he moved to the rear of the bus toward the luggage.

"Not right now," Katz answered, tugging a pearl-gray glove over the five-fingered steel prosthesis at the end of his right arm. "Mr. Johnson?"

"The medical examiner will have everything I'll need for the autopsies," James answered. "Might have to use a lab for analysis if we find anything. I don't think I'll need a piece if we're just going to the police for a while."

"You do have special weapons permits," Colonel Wells reminded them. "The governor-general told me he signed them himself."

"Yes," Katz replied. "But police officers don't care to have other people running about carrying guns."

"Part of the cop mentality," Encizo commented. "They like to think they're the only people qualified to use weapons. That's a general statement, I know, but it is largely true."

"The point is, we want cooperation with the Kingston police," Katz declared. "And we'll be more apt to get it if we don't carry any weapons when we visit their headquarters."

"Glad I'm not going there," McCarter muttered. The Briton never liked being unarmed. His Browning 9 mm pistol was holstered under his left arm beneath his sport coat.

"Try to get some rest," Katz advised. "I have a feeling we won't get much time for that later."

## 5

"I'm beginning to wonder if this whole country is going bloody bonkers," David McCarter commented as he joined the other members of Phoenix Force in Gary Manning's hotel room. "You won't believe what I heard on the news report on the radio."

"Witnesses to the most recent murders claim the killer appeared to be a zombie," Manning replied with a nod. "I heard it, too."

"Yakov and Calvin can probably tell us more than the local news," Rafael Encizo remarked as he opened an ice chest and removed a bottle of Guinness stout.

"You got any Coca-Cola in that thing?" McCarter asked; the Briton had acquired a taste for the soft drink during his tour of duty in Vietnam.

"Naturally," Encizo assured him, gesturing at the ice chest. "Coke Classic. Your favorite."

"I don't suppose you have any Moosehead?" Manning asked with a sigh.

"In Jamaica?" Encizo raised his eyebrows. "Have a pint of Guinness. So tell us what you learned from the cops."

"Not much more than we knew before," Katz confessed. "The police don't have any fascinating secret information that they've been keeping from the press. Frankly, they seem more worried about the potentially disastrous effect of the homicides on the tourist trade than about the murders themselves. It seems every segment of society in Jamaica has an opinion about the murders. A lot of the People's National Party cells are pro-Marxist and against Western democracies in general and America in particular. They don't seem too upset about the murders. A lot of Jamaican Labour Party representatives want to round up every PNP member who's ever been connected with 'radical socialist' notions. Colonel Wells himself seems to think this might not be a bad idea."

"Could be he's right," McCarter commented, pulling on the tab of his cola can.

"I disagree," Katz replied, lighting a cigarette. "I think that's a pretty drastic tactic that could result in more social unrest and stir up the sort of violence and riots that plagued Jamaica a couple years ago. Wells thinks the voodoo angle is just a smoke screen. I don't agree with that. Not after what happened at the Sir Alexander Hotel."

"The zombie killer?" Manning snorted. "Well, Cal, you took part in the autopsy. You figure the guy was a zombie?"

"Yeah," James answered, fishing in the ice chest for a beer. "You might say he was, in a way."

"God, you're joking," McCarter scoffed, surprised by his partner's reply.

"Let me tell you about this dude," James began, popping the lid off a pint of Guinness. "He looked like a walking corpse. Scrawny, bones soft from malnutrition, skin tight as a drum across his frame—and not very healthy skin at that. He was dressed in ragged clothes, smeared with dirt and crawling with maggots. I mean it: real maggots. There must've been a hundred of them stuffed into his shirt pockets. You see something like that and the first thing you'd think of would be a zombie. Right?''

''What kind of man are you talking about, Cal?'' Manning asked, clearly disgusted by the idea of someone wearing live maggots on his shirt. ''He must have been crazy.''

''Probably,'' James agreed with a nod. ''But we're not talking about everyday, ordinary, garden-variety crazy. Someone probably selected the guy, turned him into a zombie and conditioned him to kill long before there was ever a definite target....''

''Wait a minute,'' McCarter urged. ''Before I get too confused, let's clear something up. This zombie of yours wasn't a dead man brought back to life by the dark forces of voodoo or any of that rot, right?''

''No,'' James said, slightly amused by the question. ''That sucker wasn't really dead until the cops pumped five rounds into him. From the condition of the body, I don't think the poor bastard would have lived more than another week anyway.''

''That 'poor bastard' killed two innocent people,'' Gary Manning reminded him.

''I don't think he really realized what he was doing when he killed those people,'' James explained. ''There were numerous needle scars on his arms and on the soles of his feet. Most of the tracks were recent.''

"Drug addict?" Encizo asked.

"Maybe," James answered. "The dead man's liver was shot to hell, and there is a pretty good chance he had brain damage. Also, there were lots of broken blood vessels in his face and several sores on his back and chest. I'd say he was probably a chronic alcoholic: the lining of his stomach was chewed up pretty bad and looked like he'd been putting rotgut in it for years."

"Sounds like a skid-row wino," Encizo remarked.

"I think that's what he was," James confirmed. "He didn't carry any identification, of course, and I don't think anybody would even notice he'd disappeared—except maybe some of his drinking buddies on skid row. Unless they wound up the same way he did."

"What do you mean?" Manning asked, his skin crawling from listening to James's report.

"Somebody had done a number on our 'zombie,'" James explained. "There were a number of bruises and contusions around his ribs and kidneys, and the skin had been burned at his temples, at his armpits, under his nipples and on his testicles. Looked like the sort of burns caused by electrodes used for the purpose of electrical torture."

"I got a couple burn scars like that myself," Encizo commented. "Mementos of the time I was a guest in Fidel Castro's political prison. I was tortured because they wanted information and my signature on some confessions. Nobody would do that to a poor wino for those reasons.''

"Of course not," Katz agreed. "Evidently that man was tortured as part of a crude and very brutal conditioning process. Poor devil was probably already a wreck from years of alcoholism, broken in spirit and body. Then whoever worked on him used tactics similar to those a vicious trainer would use to condition a brutal attack dog.''

"They also used a lot of drugs on the guy," James added. "They're still trying to analyze traces of narcotics found in the body; so many were used it's hard to tell what they might be. Probably something was administered to break down the guy's willpower. I doubt that would be hard with a skid-row alkie.''

"Jesus," Manning muttered. "In a sense, they really *did* turn him into a zombie.''

"That brings us to the big question," McCarter said, sipping his Coke. "Who the hell are they?''

"That's why we're here," Katz remarked. "The real problem is how to find them. Rafael, you've been to Jamaica before. You have any ideas about how we should start looking for the killers?''

*"Madre de Dios,"* Encizo groaned. "I was here ten years ago, Yakov. I spent about eight months in Jamaica with a group of treasure hunters. We went diving for a Spanish galleon that had supposedly sunk somewhere off Morant Bay. The ship was supposed to be loaded with gold and jewels and all that. Never found a damn thing.''

"But you made some contacts, didn't you?" Katz asked.

"Not many," Encizo admitted. "Jamaica wasn't much of a fun place at the time. One out of three workers was unemployed. The United States and a number of other democracies had reduced economic aid and trade with Jamaica because Prime Minister Manley, who was in office at the time, was a big fan of Fidel Castro; that sure didn't endear the guy to me, either. Anyway, the economic situation was really bad back then, and it wasn't a good place for Americans to be, because a lot of Jamaicans blamed the U.S. for the mess their country was in."

"If I fall asleep in the middle of this story, just wake me up when he gets to the part about his contacts," McCarter said with an exaggerated yawn.

"I was trying to explain why the few contacts I made are probably useless now," Encizo said. "Jamaica has seen a lot of changes since then. Some of my most valuable contacts were working black-market deals at the time. I doubt if they're doing that now."

"We'll try to find them anyway," Katz told him. "Meantime, we'll have to look into the only clue that seems to keep popping up. The police are supposed to loan us one of their people who is something of an expert on the obeah voodoo groups in Kingston and the surrounding districts."

"Whoever he is, he hasn't been much help to the cops so far," McCarter growled, putting down his Coke to take a pack of Player's cigarettes from his pocket.

"We're not in a position to turn down help from any source right now," the Phoenix Force commander told him. Katz took a watch from his pocket. "Of course, we've been in Jamaica only a few hours, and we haven't done badly so far. We know a bit more about our opponents than we did before we arrived."

"I can't say I find that terribly reassuring," Manning commented. "What we've found out so far is that the enemy is even worse than we thought they were. My God, what sort of sons of bitches would turn a man into a mindless animal and then program him to kill innocent people?"

"Pretty goddamn ruthless," James said grimly. "What's worse, we'd better assume the zombie the police killed today wasn't the only one the enemy created."

"That's a cheerful thought," McCarter muttered.

"Like it or not, we'd better face that reality," Katz said, supporting James's theory. "If they can turn one poor wretch into a zombie assassin, they can do the same to others."

"How many others?" Manning asked, wishing he hadn't voiced the question the moment it had slipped from his lips.

"If they have the right equipment, enough drugs and enough subjects who meet the requirements," James said with a shrug, "hell, they might have a hundred of those things waiting to be turned loose."

6

"Mr. Gray" received a phone call from Colonel Wells at six o'clock that evening. Wells told Yakov Katzenelenbogen that Bristol and the "specialist" would be at a tavern called the Creole Dream. The colonel suggested Mr. Gray send only two of his men to meet the cops to avoid the attention a larger group might attract.

Calvin James and Rafael Encizo were the logical choices to meet Bristol and the specialist at the Creole Dream. A black man and a Hispanic man would attract less attention than any other two members of Phoenix Force. Caucasians were regarded with growing apprehension due to the rash of murders of American tourists.

Apparently many Jamaicans failed to realize that the United States of America is a great melting pot of cultures, religions and ethnic groups. That was ironic, since Jamaica is also comprised of dozens of ethnic groups. In Jamaica, the majority of the population is black or mulatto; but there are many minority groups, including East Indians, Europeans, Chinese and Hispanics.

Since the Creole Dream was located on the outskirts of Kingston in an area Wells referred to as a "shanty neighborhood," Encizo and James did not don their best summer suits for the meeting. The Cuban wore a denim jacket with matching trousers while James chose a dark blue windbreaker and a pair of khaki slacks. It was a warm evening, and neither man needed a jacket except to conceal a weapon.

Calvin James carried a Beretta 92-SB 9 mm semiautomatic pistol in shoulder leather under his left arm. A Jet-Aer G-96 fighting dagger was clipped to the Jackass Leather rig under his right arm. Rafael Encizo wore a Heckler & Koch 9 mm P9S pistol in a shoulder rig and carried a Cold Steel Tanto knife on his hip. The Cuban also had a Gerber Mark I dagger hidden in his boot. Each man carried two spare magazines for his pistol.

The Phoenix pair rode a cab to the Creole Dream. The driver seemed uncomfortable with that particular destination, which was in the shantytown beyond the city, and did not seem any happier after Encizo promised him a generous tip.

"This is not a good place to go when night has fallen, mon," the cabbie insisted. "If you wants a good time with some friendly ladies, I know a nice place near the Ocho Rios resort. Clean, friendly ladies, mon. Have you there in half an hour."

"No, thanks," Encizo replied as he and James sat in the back seat, glancing out the windows at the whitewashed buildings that seemed to form a long, pale blur in the darkness as the cab cruised through

Kingston, with little competing traffic. "Doesn't look like there's much going on tonight."

"Folks like stayin' home and prayin' it'll be a quiet night," the driver said in an ominous tone. "You chaps sound like you come here from America. Creole Dream isn't such a good place for Americans, mon...."

"How come you're so nervous, fella?" James asked. "You scared of where we're going, or are you just worried about driving around with Americans in your cab?"

"Both give me reason for concern, mon," the cabbie admitted. "You hear what happened today to that poor feller at the hotel? If I was you American fellers I'd be outta Jamaica quicker than a cat on a mouse. Not safe for you fellers right now. Ain't too good an idea to be around you fellers very long time. Look what happen to that poor maid today, mon."

"Don't worry," James chuckled. "I never heard of zombies successfully attacking a moving vehicle. Just don't park long enough for them to get together and turn over your cab and you ought to be safe."

"Laugh if you want, mon," the driver told him as the cab approached a hamlet of shabby buildings illuminated by harsh neon. "But I ain't hangin' 'round after I lets you gents outta my cab. Got me a family to look after, so I can't afford to get myself killed."

The area stank of poverty. The buildings were crudely constructed, and none stood higher than three stories. Street whores strolled along the sidewalks, watching the cab with professional interest. Winos, junkies and various breeds of burned-out humanity lurked in alleys. Other eyes watched from the windows of the surrounding buildings.

A side of Jamaica unfolded that was seldom seen by tourists. The unemployment and domestic unrest of the past two decades had been hard on the lower-income segments of Jamaican society. The slums were not mentioned by travel agents or included on vacationers' tours.

The taxi stopped in front of an ugly gray structure with faded red stripes painted across its drab surface. A neon sign above the doorway announced the home of the Creole Dream. Encizo handed the driver his fee with a large tip. The two Phoenix pros left the vehicle and the cab immediately departed, creating a mini-whirlwind of discarded newspapers and cardboard boxes in the gutter as it sped away.

"Hey, you two lookin' for a good time?" a hooker called out to the pair. She was a tall mulatto with a face as hard as concrete. "You got the money, I got what you need, mon."

"I doubt it, honey," James muttered as he and Encizo entered the Creole Dream.

The tavern was seedy and filled with smoke and the smell of sweat and stale beer. The place was dimly lit, except for a bright spotlight that shone on a crude wooden stage surrounded by tables and chairs. A black man with a shaved head occupied center stage. He was dressed only in a thin loincloth and primitive jewelry made of bones and hammered copper. The decorations were bizarre. Tiny skulls, fanglike bones and odd circular symbols hung from his neck; twisted copper snakes were wound around his ankles and wrists.

The bald man began to dance to the rhythm of the throbbing drumbeats and monotonous chanting that came from a group of performers who stood in the shadows behind him. As his contortions grew faster in time with the accelerating thunder of the drums, sweat poured down his body.

James and Encizo glanced around the rooms, adroitly and discreetly sizing up the customers at the tables, few of whom were paying attention to the strange performance on stage. Many puffed marijuana cigarettes or snorted lines of cocaine. Several bar whores were getting very friendly with male customers. James noticed one woman duck under the table beside a grinning man.

More than one set of eyes watched the Phoenix pair with suspicion. The vast majority were native Jamaicans, either black or mulatto. A few appeared to be Asian mulattoes, bronze-skinned mixed-bloods with full lips, flared nostrils, high cheekbones, straight black hair and an Oriental slant to their eyes. Nobody seemed very pleased to see the two strangers in the Creole Dream. Even the whores did not want them for clients.

At last they spotted Sergeant Bristol seated at a table at the back of the room. The Kingston cop was in the company of an attractive black woman whose hair was clipped short with black bangs combed across her forehead. The woman's eyes were large and dark, her mouth wide and sensuous. James uttered an involuntary hum of approval when he saw Bristol's companion. He and Encizo approached the table.

"You two certainly took your time getting here," Bristol complained. The cop seemed uncomfortable dressed in civilian clothes. Being surrounded by dope dealers, prostitutes, junkies and pimps did not make him any happier.

"Guess we lingered outside to enjoy the scenery," James replied, taking a chair across from Bristol and the woman. "Who's your friend?"

"Sergeant Della Walkins," she replied stiffly. "You must be Johnson. The medical examiner said you were pretty impressive at the autopsy."

"Nice to know somebody appreciated my work," James remarked. "The guy we cut up wasn't able to give his opinion."

"Are you the expert on voodoo, Miss Walkins?" Encizo inquired, joining the others at the table.

"That's what they tell me," Della answered. She tilted her head toward the stage, where now the male dancer had a live boa constrictor draped across his shoulders. "You see that?"

"Yeah," Encizo replied with a shrug. "I saw a stripper in Miami do an act similar to this with her pet snake. Frankly, I liked her performance better."

"This performance is supposed to be a ritual dance of obeah voodoo, honoring Damballah," Della explained. "It isn't a genuine ritual, of course. They wouldn't perform an actual rite for the entertainment of a bunch of louts. However, those blokes are really members of an obeah cult. This is done as a reminder to all present that voodoo still thrives in Jamaica.''

''I would have thought they'd heard enough proof of that on the news,'' James commented, watching the dancer bounce and twist with the boa constrictor wound around his neck.

''This reminds the audience that obeah is here, among them,'' Della stated. ''The eyes and ears are everywhere. If anyone talks to the authorities, the obeah cults will know about it.''

''I still think we should arrest every single member of those God-cursed devil cults,'' Bristol muttered sourly.

''That would require arresting hundreds, perhaps thousands, of cult members,'' Della told him, ''most of whom would be innocent of any crimes. Besides, voodoo isn't a form of devil worship.''

''Voodoo is a religion,'' James added. ''If you stomp out one religious group because you don't agree with it, it won't be long before the government is outlawing every faith except whatever the state approves.''

''Very good, Mr. Johnson,'' Della said approvingly.

''I have my moments,'' James grinned. ''And please call me Cal—er, it's sort of a nickname.''

''Yeah,'' Encizo muttered, worried that James might get careless around a pretty lady. It had never happened before, but there was always a first time. ''Why exactly are we here? Does all this have anything to do with our job here in Jamaica, or is this supposed to be an introduction to a crash course on obeah and voodoo?"

"A major obeah cult is located in this area," Bristol answered. "It's one that we've suspected has been dealing in cocaine and prostitution for some time. You may notice that this place is full of such activity."

"The cult is actually a cover for a criminal syndicate that uses the fear of voodoo and the occult to frighten the ignorant into obliging the hoodlums," Della added.

"What you fellers want to drink tonight?" a painfully thin waitress with long beaded hair asked as she approached the table. "Beer, rum or whiskey, mon?"

"What kind of beer?" Encizo asked.

"I look like an information center or somethin'?" the waitress said with a bored sigh. "It's bottled beer, okay? One dollar Jamaican money. Two dollars American."

"A couple beers will be fine," Encizo told her.

The waitress headed for the bar. Encizo and James exchanged glances. Both men sensed they might be in trouble. The waitress obviously figured they were Americans. If she suspected that, others in the Creole Dream probably did, too. That did not make the Phoenix pair feel very secure.

"Is there a good reason for us to hang around here?" James asked Bristol and Della. "I've got a feeling this isn't a real good place for us to be unless there's a real good reason for it."

"An informer was supposed to meet us here," Della explained. "A fella connected with the obeah cult that acts as a cover for Montgomery Penn's syndicate."

"Montgomery Penn?" Encizo asked. "Isn't he the local big shot in the Kingston underworld?"

"The biggest," Bristol answered. "We know a lot about Penn, but unfortunately we can't prove anything...."

Suddenly four men approached the table: two blacks from one side, two Asian mulattoes from the other. Their jackets were open, and at least one man carried a gun. Encizo saw the checkered grip of the revolver jutting from the man's belt.

"You didn't call for any backup, did you?" Encizo asked the two cops.

"No," Bristol answered, confused by the question.

"Oh, hell," Calvin James rasped; he had also noticed the gun.

"What—" Della began, glancing about with concern.

Returning with two beer bottles, the waitress shuffled past the Asian mulattoes without noticing anything odd about them. One of the hoods grabbed her shoulder and pulled her back. She snapped an obscenity, expressing more anger than fear. Being grabbed by men was obviously not a novelty in the Creole Dream.

"Hands off, ya bastard!" she hissed as she pulled away from the man. "Get yerself a trollop if yer John Thomas is actin' up. Plenty of sluts about..."

"Outta my way, bitch," the man growled in a soft voice that frightened her far more than an angry bellow would have.

"Thanks," Encizo declared, jumping from his chair to take the beer bottles from the waitress. "I've got them, ma'am."

Shoving the waitress aside, the hood yanked the revolver from his belt. Encizo immediately snapped his right wrist to propel a stream of beer from one bottle into the man's face. With his left hand he hammered the bottom of the other bottle into the guy's wrist. The revolver fell from numb fingers, and the hood yelped as the beer stung his eyes.

Encizo swung his right arm, slamming the bottle against the gunman's skull and hitting hard between the left ear and temple. The thug staggered sideways, dazed by the blow. The second goon threatened, aiming a stiletto with a long, thin blade at the Cuban's belly.

The Phoenix pro tossed a beer bottle at his opponent's face, distracting the knife artist. With the hard glass surface of the other bottle he deflected the blade of the stiletto. Then he grabbed the guy's wrist and twisted it, digging his fingers into the back of the thug's fist.

Pressure on the ulnar nerve forced the knifeman's fist open, and the stiletto dropped from his hand. Encizo quickly rammed an elbow stroke to the goon's chin. As the hoodlum's head snapped back, Encizo followed through with a cross-body karate chop aimed at the neck. Missing the intended target, his hand struck the guy on the side of the jaw. Nonetheless, the attacker collapsed to the floor in an inert heap.

Encizo reached inside his jacket for his H&K P9S. The first attacker, recovered from the blow with the beer bottle, suddenly swung a right cross to Encizo's jaw before the Cuban could draw his pistol. The punch sent him hurtling backward into another table. He flopped over the top, rolled with the punch and landed on his feet on the opposite side.

Shouts and screams of alarm filled the air. Customers, realizing this was more than the usual drunken donnybrook of the sort that erupted frequently in the establishment, bolted for the exits, eager to escape. Even if it had been just a knife fight, the regular patrons would have regarded the battle as entertainment, but guns had been pulled. Nobody thought it would be fun to catch a bullet.

Calvin James had been as busy as Encizo. As his partner was fighting the two Asian mulattoes, James had grabbed a chair and swung it at the nearest black thug, who had started to draw a Largo pistol from his belt. The chair hit the thug in the chest, knocking him off his feet, sending his pistol skidding across the floor; it came to rest somewhere under the wooden legs of the surrounding tables and chairs.

A second black man pulled a snubnose .38 revolver from a hip pocket. James whipped the wooden legs of the chair across the gunman's forearm, striking the revolver from his grasp. The thug responded by delivering a short left hook to the side of James's face.

Grunting with pain, the black Phoenix pro jabbed the chair legs into his opponent's chest and abdomen.

The goon staggered backward, groaning, clutching his gut. In a ruthless overhead swing, James brought the chair crashing down on his opponent's head and shoulders. Cheap and poorly made, the chair shattered on impact; so did the hoodlum's skull.

Sensing motion behind him, James glanced over his shoulder to see his first opponent rising. The Phoenix fighter executed a back kick and caught the guy between the legs with his heel. No sooner did the thug double up with a choking groan than James snapped a backfist to his face. A knuckle struck the man between the eyes, and his head rocked from the blow.

Not allowing the man time to recover, James smashed an elbow into his head. Then James smashed an elbow into his solar plexus and hooked an arm around his head. Then James jammed his shoulder under the man's chin and grabbed a fistful of hair with his other hand. Stepping forward, the Phoenix Force pro dropped to one knee and tossed the hoodlum over his shoulder. The big man sailed through space and crashed to the floor.

Sergeant Bristol rose from his chair and drew a snubnose Colt .38 from a pancake holster at the small of his back. He jammed the muzzle between the shoulder blades of the Asian mulatto who had punched Encizo across the table. The thug stiffened and raised his hands in surrender.

"Kingston police!" the sergeant announced. "You're under arrest—"

The report of a large-caliber handgun bellowed within the confines of the tavern like a baby cannon. A heavy bullet splintered wood in the wall behind Bristol. The cop flinched and unintentionally triggered his Colt revolver. A 148-grain solid-ball slug ripped through the spinal cord of his prisoner. The high-velocity bullet bored a dime-sized exit wound in the man's chest. The thug's eyes opened wide in astonishment as his lifeless body fell to the floor.

"Oh, my God!" Bristol exclaimed, stunned that he had shot an unarmed man in the back.

Bristol was too startled to realize that someone had tried to shoot him. He stared, motionless, at the man he had accidentally executed. An easy target, he probably would have been picked off by the enemy gunman if Encizo and Della Walkins hadn't turned their attention toward the muzzle flash that had appeared at the edge of the stage.

One of the drummers from the phony obeah voodoo act had fired at Bristol. His weapon had been a .45 caliber Colt 1911-A1 pistol. Luckily for the police sergeant, the man was a poor marksman. He didn't get another chance to waste Bristol. Rafael Encizo drew his Heckler & Koch autoloader, snap-aimed, and fired two rounds into the enemy gunman.

Both 9 mm parabellum slugs ripped into the gunman's chest. One bullet punched his breastbone into shards of internal shrapnel that carved into heart and lungs. The other messenger of death hit directly in the life pump. The gunman dropped his .45 Colt and fell back against the stage, dead.

Encizo, just as he was firing his H&K piece, glimpsed another figure beside the stage, and instinctively ducked behind the cover of a table and chairs. A split second later, another gun roared, and a slug pierced the tabletop above the Cuban's head. It narrowly missed his left shoulder as it sizzled past and burrowed into the floorboards near his left knee.

*"¡Cristo!"* he exclaimed, his teeth clenched as the close brush with a lethal chunk of hot flying lead sent a familiar tremor up his spine.

By then, Sergeant Della Walkins had taken a .38 Colt from her purse. She gripped the snubgun in a two-handed Weaver's stance and triggered two shots at the second gunman. Another voodoo drummer screamed and staggered into the open, a Star pistol still in his fist.

Bloodstains streaked the gunman's yellow T-shirt. Two .38 slugs had pierced the man's upper torso, but he was still on his feet. As the wounded man started to raise his weapon, Della shot him again. The third slug was charmed. Now no more than food for worms, the guy toppled backward and hit the floor.

Suddenly the bald and all-but-naked figure of the obeah dancer, reappearing on stage, shrieked at the Phoenix pair and their police allies, and began to whirl his boa constrictor overhead by its tail like a reptilian lasso. He hurled the deadly serpent at Della, who screamed and leaped away. The snake, hissing and squirming, landed on a table near the lady cop. Instinctively she fired her pistol at the reptile. Her bullet missed and punched through the wood near the snake's thick, coiled body.

The dancer scooped up the .45 pistol discarded by one of the slain drummers and aimed the weapon at the distressed and distracted Della Walkins. With his Beretta 92-SB, which he had by then unsheathed, Calvin James lined up the sights on the head of the dancer and squeezed the trigger. A single slug smashed into the hairless dome. The man's head recoiled as the bullet drilled through his skull. His corpse wilted to the floor without uttering a whisper of protest.

"You okay, Della?" James called out as he moved toward her.

She bolted forward, hugged him. She was trembling slightly as James wrapped an arm around her, unable to resist a grin. She felt good. The warmth of her body, the pressure of her breasts against his rib cage, reminded James that he had not been with a woman for a long time. Too long.

"That was the last of them," Encizo announced, but he did not holster his weapon. "Everybody okay?"

"My God," Bristol said, still looking at the man he had shot in the back. "What have I done?"

"Get a hold of yourself, damn it!" Encizo snapped. "We don't have time to put up with any hysterics. There could be more of them outside. Don't worry about that damn snake, either. Boa constrictors aren't poisonous and the only time one ever crushed a person to death was in the movies."

"I know," Della said, obviously embarrassed. She slowly released Calvin James. "Sorry. I guess it just startled me when he threw that snake...."

"We were all kinda startled," James assured her, smiling at the pretty lady cop. "You did just fine, and I didn't mind the fact you wound up in my arms. Like to do it again under different circumstances."

She wasn't certain how to respond, but a sly smile betrayed her feelings. "Maybe we'll see about that later...."

"That's real nice, you two," Encizo remarked as he approached and flattened a dazed opponent who was starting to get to his feet, "but we got a couple of live prisoners to collect before we leave here."

"Always something comes along to ruin the mood," James muttered sourly.

## 7

"Your people certainly play rough, Mr. Gray," Colonel Wells remarked as he met with Yakov Katzenelenbogen, Gary Manning and David McCarter in Lieutenant Farley Smith's office at Kingston police headquarters. "They killed five men at the Creole Dream."

"Service must be pretty lousy there," McCarter said with a shrug. The Briton was in a surly mood because he had missed the first battle with the enemy. McCarter thrived on action, and he always resented it when he did not get to participate.

"I don't find this amusing, Mr. Carver," Lieutenant Smith declared tensely. He was a white Jamaican, a descendant of a long line of British colonials, but he did not seem to care much for the commando from Mother England. "We've had more than our share of violence in Jamaica, but we don't take it lightly."

"So you fret about it bloody well," McCarter replied, meeting Smith's glare without flinching. "What else do you do, mate? Have conferences to discuss the effects of violence on society? Sit on your arse having tea and crumpets while the bastards are running around free..."

"Mr. Personality strikes again," Manning snorted, pouring some black coffee into a cup.

"Take it easy, Mr. Carver," Katz told McCarter. The Phoenix Force commander had quietly read through the incident reports written by Sergeants Bristol and Walkins. "As for you, Lieutenant Smith, I suggest you take a look at these. Two of your fellow police officers confirm that our friends acted in self-defense. In fact, they both agree that Johnson and Sanchez probably saved their lives during the gun battle with the 'unidentified assailants.' If you expect my men to agree to get themselves killed instead of defending themselves because it upsets you, then you're a damn fool, and we don't have time to waste with such nonsense."

"You act as if you and your people were in charge here," Smith huffed, jutting out his lower lip until it nearly touched the tip of his hawkish nose. "This isn't your country—"

"But they are in charge of this operation," Colonel Wells told the police lieutenant in a flat, hard voice. "The governor-general and the prime minister agreed to this unorthodox chain of command due to a direct request by the President of the United States."

"Why should Jamaica have to oblige the American President?" Smith demanded.

"Because the United States happens to be the most powerful and influential government and country in this hemisphere," Katz replied. "Whether you like it or not, that's the way the world is, Lieutenant. Your government doesn't want to be on bad terms with the

U.S., so they've agreed to cooperate with the President's wishes. We get our authority from the Oval Office, so our presence here is the President's wish at this time.''

"I can't place your accent," Smith told Katz, "but it doesn't sound like you're from the United States. This Carver character or whatever his real name might be sounds like a cockney thug from an East London slum.''

"Been to my old neighborhood, Smitty?" McCarter asked with a twisted smile that would have looked right at home on the face of an ax murderer. "I doubt that. They would've chewed you up and spit you out, you prissy little bastard.''

"This is bullshit," Manning announced in a serious tone. "I'm about ready to knock their heads together. What's really important isn't who is in charge or how many low-life hoodlums got killed in a gunfight tonight. No innocent bystanders got hurt, and neither your officers nor our partners were injured. That's not bad news. The fact that two enemies were taken captive could be our first big break in this assignment.''

"They weren't 'taken prisoner,'" Smith corrected. "They were placed under arrest by the Kingston Police Department. Unfortunately, Sergeant Bristol admits in his report that he shot an unarmed suspect point-blank in the back and killed him. Bristol will be suspended from duty until that matter has been investigated and the department decides what action to take against him.''

"He'd never been in a firefight before," McCarter declared. "Bristol's reaction to being shot at is pretty understandable under the circumstances. The bloke could have claimed the bastard tried to whirl about and disarm him. Instead, Bristol told you the truth. I think that took a lot of guts."

"The conduct of our police officers is not your concern, Carver," Smith told him. "We are still entitled to decide that much about our own department...or has the American President taken over that as well?"

"Please, gentlemen," Colonel Wells urged, holding his pudgy hands up to get their attention. "We're getting away from the important issues here. We must learn if these gunmen are members of the conspiracy to murder Americans in Jamaica, or if tonight's incident was simply some sort of hideous coincidence."

"Mr. Johnson is presently trying to determine if the two prisoners are in sound medical condition to be interrogated under the influence of scopolamine," Katz stated. "The drug is a very powerful truth serum and can be lethal if improperly used or if the subject has any sort of heart trouble or other ailment."

"I don't think it's legal to use such a drug," Smith said, turning to Wells. "Are you going to let them do this?"

"They are in charge, Lieutenant," Wells reminded him. "Does Johnson know what he's doing with this truth serum?"

"He's used it many times in the past," Katz assured the colonel. "Johnson has never lost a patient under the influence of scopolamine. If he has any doubts, he won't even attempt to use it."

A knock on the door interrupted the conversation. Smith asked who it was, and "Johnson" and "Sanchez" identified themselves. The lieutenant opened the door to allow Calvin James and Rafael Encizo to enter the office.

"Well," James began as he sat on the edge of Smith's desk. "I won't be giving either one of those dudes any injections to make them chatty for us. Neither man is a safe subject. They're both heavy cigarette smokers, and they've both been using cocaine pretty regularly for at least a year. A dose of scopolamine would probably kill either man rather than make him talk."

"One of them did say something," Encizo announced as he helped himself to the coffee. "It's sort of crazy, but it sure is interesting."

"What are you waiting for?" McCarter asked impatiently. "Background music? What did the bastard say?"

"He said nothing we could do would make him talk," Encizo explained, "because Cercueil would know if he talked or not. Cercueil, he said, can read minds and see into the future. He can protect our little jailbird with his *bocor* magic or kill him with a juju curse."

"Cercueil?" Manning stared at Encizo. "That's impossible."

"That guy doesn't think so," the Cuban replied. "He really believes Cercueil is aware of everything that happens on this island, and that he can really carry out this supernatural stuff. He thinks Cercueil can destroy him. He's afraid of a slow and painful death. Then his corpse could be turned into a slave and his soul cast into some very nasty region of voodoo hell. I don't know what we can threaten him with, but it'll be pretty hard to top that."

"But Cercueil can't be behind this," Manning insisted.

"Cercueil?" Smith asked, confused by the conversation.

"Maurice Cercueil," Katz explained. "He was formerly the head of the Ton Ton Macoute under Papa Doc Duvalier. After the old man died, Cercueil created a terrorist network in the United States known as the Black Alchemists. They managed to infiltrate production lines of food-processing companies, cosmetics and tobacco products and sabotage the goods with poisons and acids. More than a dozen people were injured and killed by these vicious and ruthless terrorists."

"Why did they do such terrible things?" Wells asked.

"Cercueil tried to blackmail the U.S. government into giving him arms and money," Manning answered. "Probably planned to go back to Haiti and overthrow Jean-Claude Duvalier and put himself in charge. Whatever his final plan, he didn't live to carry it out."

"Are you sure he's dead?" Smith inquired with his absurd pouting frown. "Did you actually see the body, or is this all information you read in intelligence reports?"

"Maurice Cercueil is dead," Calvin James assured him. "I killed him myself. Is that good enough?"

"If you're positive you killed him," Smith answered.

"The sonuvabitch is dead," James sighed. "I cut his head off, for God's sake. That's about as dead as you can get."

"But you didn't stuff the mouth with salt and sew it shut to make sure Cercueil didn't stick his head back on and come back to life," McCarter snickered.

"That's not funny," Wells told him.

"Cercueil isn't a goddamn zombie, either," McCarter snorted as he started to pace the office floor. "It's bloody obvious some other bastard has taken over Cercueil's identity and they've revived the Black Alchemists—or something just like it."

"Wouldn't be the first time something like that happened," Manning was forced to agree. "Everybody figured the Baader-Meinhof gang was dead after both leaders committed suicide and terrorism in West Germany seemed to taper off a bit in the late seventies. Then nine American military bases were sabotaged in 1981, and the Baader-Meinhof gang took credit for it."

"Let's look at what we've learned so far," Katz began, placing a Camel cigarette between the tridentlike hooks of the prosthesis at the end of his right arm. It was his favorite device, more obvious than the five-fingered prosthesis, perhaps, but also far more practical. "Since at least one of the hoods apparently really believes in voodoo, there is a genuine connection here. Not just a front."

"Agreed," Encizo stated. "Cercueil's name suggests Haitians are involved. I doubt if many people outside Haiti would be familiar with the former boss of the Ton Ton Macoute. Probably members of the Haitian secret police are part of the outfit."

"Well," James commented, "Haiti is pretty close to Jamaica, and the Ton Ton Macoute had good reason to flee Haiti in a hurry when Jean-Claude Duvalier went down the tubes. God knows the Haitian people had plenty of old scores to settle with the secret police. Any Ton Ton storm trooper who wanted to stay alive would get the hell out of the country PDQ. Closest places to run would be the Dominican Republic, Cuba and Jamaica."

"They wouldn't want to go to Cuba," Encizo remarked. "Castro would probably send them to Angola."

"I assume you've got information on Haitian refugees currently living in Jamaica?" Manning asked Colonel Wells. "That might be a good place to start looking for the new Cercueil."

"How far back should this material cover?" Wells responded, frowning. "The last two years or the last twenty? The Duvaliers were in power for quite a while."

"Concentrate on refugees who came here after the fall of Baby Doc's rule or a couple of months earlier," Manning answered. "That would probably be the most likely time Ton Ton Macoute fugitives would have fled to Jamaica. If that doesn't produce anything promising, we'll have to check refugees and immigrants before and since that date.''

"That's going to be a tiresome task that will probably fail to produce anything at all,'' Smith muttered.

"My office will deal with it, Lieutenant,'' Wells told him. "We have computer operators who specialize in this sort of thing. That's why we have tons of trivial data stored in the computer memory banks. Of course, you realize these Haitians may have entered the country illegally, and then we wouldn't have any record of them at all.''

"Still worth a try,'' Encizo stated. "For now, I think we ought to get some sleep. People trying to kill me and forcing me to fight to stay alive always wear me out a little. I know I should be used to it by now, but I guess I'll never really earn that superman badge. I admit I still do get a little upset when somebody tries to rearrange my brains with a bullet.''

None of the members of Phoenix Force would argue with Encizo. They felt the same way, and not one had come as close to sudden death by a high-velocity projectile as the Cuban had when a 9 mm slug had creased his skull during a previous mission. Encizo had been laid up in a USAEUR military hospital in West Germany for several months before he had been fit for duty. Obviously, that wasn't an experience he wanted to go through again. Of course, the odds of surviving another bullet to the skull were somewhere between slim and Rest In Peace.

"Good idea," Katz agreed. "I think we should all get some rest and tackle this again in the morning."

"Are Bristol and Della Walkins getting the rest of the night off?" James asked Lieutenant Smith. "I saw them out in the corridor. They looked like they weren't sure whether to leave or not."

"Sergeant Walkins can leave," Smith declared. "Bristol may as well go home for now, too. We'll have to decide what to do with him later."

"Bristol hasn't exactly won any personality contests with us, Lieutenant," James remarked, "but he didn't murder that suspect in the bar. He had his gun in the guy's back. A bullet whistled past his ear and he pulled the trigger. You so sure you wouldn't have done the same thing under those circumstances?"

"It's a department matter, Mr. Johnson," Smith replied stiffly. "However, I can assure you that you won't be working with Sergeant Bristol in the field again."

"Are you sure that's a wise decision?" Katz inquired, blowing a smoke ring across the room. "We have to keep a low profile, and we can't have every cop in Kingston involved with this mission. Bristol was chosen because he was familiar with one of the homicide incidents involving American tourists. That's the same reason you were chosen to assist us, Lieutenant. If you have another officer to replace Bristol, I must remind you that this individual should already be familiar with the incidents that brought us here. He or she must also have top-secret clearance from the governor-general's office and be familiar with all parts of

Kingston and other parts of the island. Unless you have a suitable replacement, we'd like Sergeant Bristol to remain with our unit for now. For security reasons."

"You men must be used to getting your own way," Smith said through clenched teeth.

"We try," Katz replied unapologetically. "Look at it this way, Lieutenant. If we get our way throughout this mission, the terrorists don't get their way. If we're really dealing with the Black Alchemists or an outfit just like them, you'd better pray our side wins. The fate of the entire nation of Jamaica might depend on the outcome."

8

Della Walkins lived in an apartment building near the Jamaican College of Arts, Science and Technology. Calvin James spotted the educational complex from her terrace. Moonlight cast a soft glow on the thirty-year-old college. The view was disturbed only by the swaying tops of palm trees and the glare of street-lights below.

A cool breeze drifted through the night, carrying the fresh ocean scent of the Caribbean. There was little traffic that night, and the streets were quiet. Kingston seemed a peaceful and pleasant city as James stood on the terrace. The distant sound of calypso music floated through the air, the music softer than the rattling of ice cubes in the drink Della had handed him before she had disappeared into the bedroom.

James took a sip and grimaced. Whatever it was, it didn't please him; it tasted as if somebody had charred a hickory stick and stirred it in rubbing alcohol. But since Della had made the drink for him, he could live with it…as long as he didn't actually have to drink it.

"Enjoying the view?" she asked as she emerged from the bedroom and stepped onto the terrace. James turned to face her. A white terry-cloth robe was tied around her narrow waist, revealing the round curves of her dark brown breasts. The hem of the robe was short enough to show off her well-shaped legs and firm ebony thighs.

"The view's great from here," James answered with a smile. "How are you doing now that you've had a chance to relax a bit after all the excitement?"

"I've been a police officer for several years, Cal," she answered. "It really wasn't because I was so terribly distressed about what happened at the Creole Dream that I let you bring me home."

"I didn't figure you were really rattled by that," James replied, stepping closer. "You handled yourself pretty well. You're a very impressive lady, in more ways than one."

"Really?" she smiled. "You've barely touched that drink. Don't you care for gin and tonic?"

"So that's what this is." James glanced at the glass in his hand and frowned. "I thought maybe it was used to thin paint or something."

"I'll take it," Della said. "I should have guessed gin and tonic was something an American might not care for. Popular here, of course, because of the British influence, I imagine. Would you care for a beer or a rum and soda instead?"

"Either sounds fine," he assured her. James watched the woman cross the room to the bar of her kitchenette. "Hey, did you attend the college out there?"

"Arts, Science and Technology?" Della replied as she took a bottle of beer from the refrigerator. "No, I attended the University of the West Indies in Mona. That's a suburb of Kingston. I couldn't afford to live there on a police sergeant's salary. Going to university there was expensive, of course, but my mummy and daddy insisted. I was supposed to be a sociologist or an anthropology professor or something intellectual. My parents weren't terribly happy when I left college and entered the police academy. I suppose they still aren't very pleased about that."

"Parents always want their kids to do things they never could," James commented, walking to the kitchen as Della approached with the beer in one hand and the gin and tonic in the other. "They have dreams for their children and sometimes forget kids have their own dreams. I'm sure your parents will realize you have to do what you want with your life. It is *your* life, after all."

"Oh, I think they're accepting it...gradually," Della said. She handed him the beer. "What are your parents like?"

"They were hardworking people who didn't get many breaks," James answered with a shrug. "They were poor, and they had a lot of problems caused by racial discrimination. Fortunately, they lived to see things change for the better and even helped to make some of those changes happen. My father died shortly after two of his sons went off to Vietnam; he never knew only one would come back. My mom was killed by muggers...hell, I don't really want to talk about that."

"I'm sorry," Della told him, steering James toward the couch. "Sounds like you've had a rather hard time growing up, then Vietnam and all the other things that led you to do whatever it is you do now. You and your friends are very mysterious, Cal."

"I can't tell you much about that," James said as he sat beside her. "Don't ask. Usually I have to tell a lot of people a lot of lies in my profession. I've been pretty up-front with you, and I'd like to keep it that way."

"No questions," she agreed, sipping her gin and tonic. "Well, I do have one. When you asked if you could see me home tonight—was that just because you were worried that I was upset about the shooting and the snake and all that rot?"

"That was part of it," James replied, putting down his beer to take one of her hands in his. "But that wasn't the only reason, and I think you know it. You're not only beautiful, you're also bright and appealing. That's a very attractive combination."

"I don't generally bring men up here," Della began, glancing down at the ice cubes floating in her glass. "Especially not a man I've known for less than a day. After what happened tonight, though, I realize we might both be killed before it's over. Even if we both survive, you'll go back to the States when this is finished. So right now might be all the time we have...."

James placed a hand on her cheek and gently turned her face toward his. He kissed her on the lips; a gentle, brief kiss. When she responded, he kissed her again, his tongue sliding across her teeth and probing the roof of her mouth.

They embraced as their hands made tentative sallies across each other's bodies. Della untied her robe; she was naked beneath the terry cloth. James caressed a breast gently, feeling the rigid nipple between his fingers. Della slid a hand inside his shirt and ran it across the hard muscles of his chest.

She stripped off his shirt as he stroked her long, smooth thighs. For a long time they feverishly held each other, trying to get as close as possible. There was no need for words when he finally heaved himself above her, only Della's willing compliance as they joined in the ultimate intimacy.

THE FOLLOWING MORNING, Calvin James and Della Walkins arrived at Kingston police headquarters together. Colonel Wells, Lieutenant Smith and the other members of Phoenix Force were waiting for them in the homicide investigator's office.

"I'm so glad you managed to join us, Mr. Johnson," Katz remarked. The hard stare he fixed on James's face suggested to the black commando that the Phoenix Force commander was somewhat less than pleased.

"How's everybody doing today?" James asked with a weak grin. He knew he would get an ass-chewing from Yakov later. The hell with it, he thought. It had been worth it to spend the night with Della.

"I managed to contact an old acquaintance I knew when I was in Jamaica on those treasure-hunting trips of my youth," Rafael Encizo explained. "The fellow is in a bit of trouble with the government right now—he hasn't paid any taxes for about two decades. They're demanding he either comes up with about six hundred thousand dollars or goes to jail for about a hundred years. Unless he can make a deal with the governor-general's office."

"Can't say I approve of this sort of thing, Mr. Sanchez," Colonel Wells remarked. "Making deals with criminals doesn't seem right to me. This man Kevinson is a smuggler as well as a tax evader. Not the sort of person I regard as trustworthy."

"Todd Kevinson *is* a smuggler," Encizo agreed. "Cigars, rum, curios and stuff like that. He's never dealt in drugs or gunrunning. Kevinson is hardly a tribute to good citizenship, but he's far from a threat to the national security of Jamaica. If he can arrange for us to meet Montgomery Penn, it will be worth making a deal with the guy."

"I still say we arrest Penn and make him talk," Smith declared. "I guess you were right to want to use that truth serum and make him tell us where to find these Ton Ton Macoute scum."

"That idea is fine up to a point," Katz began, gesturing with his trident hook. "Kevinson can tell us where to find Penn, but he can't tell us anything about what sort of security the gangster will have. That could mean a bloodbath. Also, Penn has a number of lawyers who've kept him out of jail every time you've arrested him in the past. They'd probably be contacted the moment you snapped the cuffs on the guy. They'd be here waiting for him before we got him back to the department."

"We could always take him somewhere else, give him scopolamine in a more private setting," Mc-Carter suggested, lighting up a Player's cigarette. "No need for those shyster legal eagles to know a damn thing."

"And have the Kingston police accused of kidnapping?" Smith snorted. "I think not, Carver."

"The last point is probably the most important," Katz continued. "Since Penn isn't a Haitian, I'm sure the Ton Ton Macoute isn't going to trust him with any more details than they have to. We may not learn anything of any earthshaking importance from him. Sure, he probably knows dozens of low-level hoods involved, but he may not even know where the Cercueil impostor and the other real leaders are located. Even if he does know, they'll most likely abandon their headquarters as soon as they learn Penn's been arrested."

"Do you really think this plan of yours has a better chance of success?" Wells demanded. "It sounds very dangerous and risky, in my opinion."

"Excuse me," James began sheepishly. "Can I hear the plan?"

"What do you say, fellas?" Manning asked the others. "Should we let him in on it, even if he did arrive late?"

"Okay," Encizo began, in a more serious voice. "Todd Kevinson has done business with Penn; smuggling Jamaican cigars to Florida, for instance, and passing them off as Havana-made in order to get a higher price. Anyway, Kevinson knows enough about Penn's operations to know the gangster has been trying to get a covert connection with a banking corporation in the Lesser Antilles for about two years."

"Lesser Antilles?" James raised his eyebrows.

"The Antilles Islands," Katz explained. "Most are still dependencies of the Netherlands, France or the United Kingdom. Until recently, they were best known for petroleum, phosphates and tourism. Lately they've become a popular spot for individuals and organizations who want a secure bank account."

"Like the kind of secret Swiss bank accounts the mob and crooked politicians are fond of?" James asked.

"Swiss bank accounts aren't what they used to be," Gary Manning told him, pouring the last of a pot of coffee into his cup, and frowning as black grounds spilled into the Styrofoam container. "Pressure from several governments, law-enforcement agencies and other international organizations have convinced the Swiss in recent years to alter their secret banking policies. The accounts aren't so secret anymore."

"Same thing happened to the banking business in the Cayman Islands," David McCarter added. "That had been a favorite place for American mobsters to launder money and for cocaine syndicates to stash away cash in secret accounts. But the United States and England complained long enough and loud enough until the Cayman Islands decided doing banking for crooks wasn't worth the heat they were getting. Besides, the Cayman Islands are still technically a British dependency."

"So that leaves the Antilles Islands as the favorite spot for crooks to deposit their money for safekeeping," Encizo supplied. "Panama is very popular, too, especially among the cocaine syndicates of South America. Penn doesn't want his money that far away, and he's been trying to get a supersecret account in the Antilles. He doesn't want to go through regular channels for fear he'll run into trouble with the authorities. The Antilles' banking businesses are currently under the same sort of pressure the Swiss and the Cayman Islands experienced in the past. Getting so criminals just can't save a dishonest dollar."

"Okay," James began. "I think I get the picture now. We're going to pretend to be representatives from some bank from the Antilles Islands. We promise him a secret bank account with ten percent interest, a free calendar, and a chance for a great savings plan for retirement."

"Something like that," Katz confirmed. "Kevinson says he'll gladly arrange for us to meet with Penn and help us with our cover in return for amnesty by the governor-general's office for withholding taxes all these years."

"A hundred things could go wrong with a plan like that," Smith warned. "Penn isn't a fool. It won't be easy to convince him you blokes are genuine."

"It's risky," Katz agreed. "But it's also the best way to get close to Penn and learn enough about the bastard to see if he can lead us to Cercueil. If nothing else, we should be able to get enough information to make an arrest stick when you nail Penn later.''

"Who's going to take part in this little masquerade?" James inquired.

"I planned to play the banker," Katz answered. "Would you like to be one of my bodyguards, Mr. Johnson? I realize you have a busy social life, but perhaps you could manage to squeeze this into your schedule."

"I'll do it, man," James assured him, embarrassed by Katz's sarcasm, although he realized he deserved it.

"That's nice," the Israeli said dryly. He turned to Gary Manning. "Do you want to join us, Mr. Green?"

"Sure," the Canadian replied with a shrug. "Which one of the Antilles are we supposed to be from?"

"A French dependency," Katz answered. "All three of us speak French fluently."

"I speak French, too," McCarter declared, worried he might miss out on the action again. "Why not take three bodyguards?"

"Three reasons," Katz answered. "First, two bodyguards wouldn't seem suspicious. More than that will probably make Penn a bit uncomfortable. Second, I didn't choose Green and Johnson just because they speak French. With his background in business and foreign trade, Green might be able to help me convince Penn we're really with a shady banking outfit. And Johnson is a logical choice because blacks are the largest ethnic group of both Guadeloupe and Martinique; three white faces might seem a bit odd.

Finally, I want you and Sanchez to head a backup team in case we get in trouble. Make sense?''

"I suppose so," McCarter said with a sigh.

"Cheer up," Encizo said, patting the Briton on the back. "You'll get to shoot somebody eventually. I suggest you guys claim to be from Martinique. It isn't as big as Guadeloupe, but it attracts more casino crowds, and it's more likely to offer the sort of banking deals which would appeal to Penn."

"Good idea," Katz agreed. "We'll brush up on Martinique while you contact Kevinson and find out how soon we get to meet Kingston's Al Capone."

"Just a moment," Colonel Wells began. "You gentlemen can't be serious. This isn't a strong enough plan of action to possibly be successful."

Della, who had been silent since entering the room, aware that Lieutenant Smith was probably as upset with her as Katz appeared to be with Calvin James, now added, "The colonel has a point. Perhaps you should plan this more carefully."

"We really can't plan much more until we find out where and when we'll be meeting with Penn," Katz explained. "We'll work out the details when we know enough to make the rest of our strategy. Now, if you'll excuse me, I'd like to have a few words in private with Mr. Johnson."

"Oh, shit," James rasped under his breath.

The two Phoenix Force members left the office, and headed up the corridor to an exit. James kept his mouth shut and followed Katz to the door. The Israeli led him outside into the parking lot, past a row of police cars.

James was anxious, eager to get the ass-chewing over with. Not one to take any chances, Katz did not speak until he was certain they were out of earshot of any of Kingston's finest. He even turned his back to the police building in case Smith or Wells had a lip-reader with a pair of binoculars posted at a window.

"Did you have a good time with Sergeant Walkins last night?" Katz inquired, taking a pack of Camels from his pocket.

"I know what you're gonna say, Yakov," James told him.

"Really?" Katz raised his eyebrows. "Then you realize you violated our security last night? You left with that woman without telling any of us where you were going. If we had needed you, if there had been an emergency, we would have been unable to contact you. Rafael guessed you were probably with Sergeant Walkins. You two seem to have had a real attraction for each other from the moment you met."

"It won't happen again," James assured him.

"We can't afford any emotional involvement during a mission, Cal," Katz warned. "You don't know her well enough to trust her. You have to keep your mind on the mission. Don't you remember what happened in the Bahamas when you wound up in bed with that woman from the casino?"

"I remember," James said with a nod.

"You almost got killed that time," Katz stated, lighting a cigarette. "I would have thought that would have taught you a lesson. We can't afford to be short-handed during a mission. It's not just your life you put at risk when you're operating at less than peak level. Phoenix Force is a team, and we have to function like one. Each of us has to be able to rely on the others to do their jobs at all times. Understand?''

"Yeah," James replied. "I fucked up."

"Well..." Katz took a long draw on his cigarette. "There wasn't any real harm done, except perhaps that Wells and Smith might have a little less confidence in us now than they did before. I don't think they were exactly bubbling over with faith in us before this happened.''

"I didn't tell Della anything, Yakov," James stated. "She didn't pry about details, either. It was really just between the two of us. Just for the one night.''

"You know, we're all human, Cal," the Israeli said with a sigh. "I don't really blame you. She's a lovely lady. This just isn't the time for it.''

"Never is," James muttered. "When I joined Phoenix Force, I didn't figure we'd be on a mission every other month. We use so many phony names I'm not sure what to call you guys half the time. Sometimes I'm not sure what name *I'm* supposed to respond to. Worse than that, sometimes I'm not even sure who or *what* I am anymore.''

"Yes, I know that feeling," Katz said with a nod. "I've been doing this sort of thing since before you were born, Cal. I've been doing it so long it seems like a normal way of life.''

"Sometimes I don't feel like I'm a person anymore," James explained. "Brognola tells us to go to some country. Turkey, Greece, France, Finland or Mongolia, for God's sake. The only place that looks familiar anymore is the War Room back at Stony Man headquarters. Whether we're in Kenya or the Vatican or here in Jamaica, it's always the same. We run around telling lies to people we barely know and only work with for a few days. Then we wind up getting shot at and generally killing a bunch of people who are supposed to be bad guys. But I see so little of what we're supposed to be defending, I'm not always sure what the hell it is anymore."

Katz shrugged. "I think we all feel that way sometimes. Except maybe McCarter. That's one man who'd be lost without a battlefield. Perhaps we're all like that to a degree, or we wouldn't be doing this. The only thing that makes any sense is that we're fighting for some very important things. Freedom and civilization can seem pretty hard to grasp when you're always in the trenches with a gun in your hand."

"Yeah," James replied. "But I guess we see enough of what the other side does to know they can't be right. Maybe I should say the other *sides*."

"Evil has more than one face," Katz remarked.

"This time," James added, "it belongs to some bastard calling himself Cercueil. Whoever he is, he poisons innocent people, turns burned-out winos into brain-damaged killers and God knows what else. We sure as hell can't let him get away with that sort of stuff."

"Then let's get inside," Katz suggested. "We still have a lot of work to do."

**9**

Spanish Town is a unique relic of Jamaica's earliest history. The Spanish first settled in Jamaica in the early 1500s, when they began the cultivation of the sugarcane crop and the exploitation of slaves imported from Africa. Later, in 1655, the British captured the island, and thereafter influenced its culture, language and customs.

However, the influence of the original Spanish settlers—the Arawak Indians who were indigenous to Jamaica seldom get any sort of official recognition—can still be found in Spanish Town. Adobe buildings with whitewashed walls and red tile rooftops can still be found here. Spanish restaurants are popular, and calypso music is frequently sung in Spanish; some say it closely resembles the music of Trinidad and Tobago.

The mansion three kilometers from Spanish Town reflected a Spanish style of architecture. The hacienda, sometimes referred to as "the Palace of Madrid," belonged to Gabriel Carlos de Madrid, a wealthy sugarcane-plantation owner. His mulatto family heritage claimed to be part Spanish, part Arawak, and part Maroon—a term given to the original freed slaves of Jamaica. The family swore that de Madrid was their genuine family name. No one could prove it was not true, and few honestly cared much one way or the other. The rich are entitled to eccentric names if it makes them happy.

Sugarcane had always been a major crop in Jamaica, especially since it was used in making rum. Gabriel Carlos de Madrid had made a fortune selling sugarcane to refineries and to legal exporters. It was believed he had also made a secret second fortune by supplying sugarcane to Montgomery Penn for black market bootleg booze, most of which found its way to the United States.

A party was in progress at the Palace of Madrid that night, and the three bankers from Martinique were invited. A long black limousine pulled up to the great adobe hacienda. Rafael Encizo, clad in a dark blue chauffeur's uniform, sat behind the steering wheel. Calvin James, Yakov Katzenelenbogen and Gary Manning were seated in the back of the big luxury vehicle. James wished he could loosen the black bow tie at his throat. He was not accustomed to formal clothing. Gary Manning appeared to be equally uncomfortable in white dinner jacket and tie. The unflappable Katzenelenbogen seemed to accept the costume with ease. It took more than a bow tie to ruffle the Israeli's feathers.

"Jesus," James muttered, gazing through the tinted glass of the limo at the great house illuminated by floodlights. "This de Madrid dude not only has it, he knows how to flaunt it, too."

"Yeah," Manning agreed as he watched two large black men dressed in red tuxedo jackets approach the car. "Here comes the welcome wagon."

"Let's go," Katz declared, reaching for the door handle. "We don't want them to search this limo."

"Good luck, amigos," Encizo urged. "Watch your ass in there. The place is probably crawling with snakes who walk on two legs."

"I hope so," Katz said with a faint smile. "Otherwise, this trip is a waste of time." James, Katz and Manning emerged from the car.

The men in red jackets politely asked to see their invitations. Katz handed a passport with a note sticking from it to one of the men. He noticed that the other guy's jacket was open, and a strip of leather was visible at his shoulder, part of a holster rig. Music played within the mansion, and the murmur of dozens of voices carried to the front court outside.

"I believe this should satisfy Mr. de Madrid," Katz stated. "He is expecting us, *oui*?"

"Henri Picard," the bodyguard remarked, reading the passport. The identification papers were excellent forgeries, printed by the French Sûreté for Phoenix Force for a previous mission. In fact, everything was genuine except the fingerprints, names and ID numbers.

"It is a French passport," Katz explained, easily adopting a Parisian accent, "and, as you may note, I have been living and working in Martinique for the last twelve years. I am a banker."

"Oh, yes," the man said, smiling as he returned the passport. "Mr. de Madrid told us to expect you. Please follow me."

Encizo drove the limo around the horseshoe-shaped driveway and headed out the exit gate. The two bodyguards in red watched the car depart. So did several men dressed as chauffeurs who were clustered about a row of expensive automobiles parked in the front court. These included two limos, three or four Mercedeses, a number of BMWs and at least one Rolls-Royce. The men of Phoenix Force could not see the line of cars well enough to count them or determine what sort of autos made up the collection of rich men's toys.

"Your driver could have waited," the bodyguard remarked. "The other guests' cars and drivers are staying until the party is over."

"The limousine is a rental," Katz explained. "So is the driver. We told him to leave after bringing us here and not to return until ten o'clock. I'm certain we'll have completed our business by then."

"I see," the man said, nodding. "One can't be too careful, eh?"

"A wise philosophy," Katz agreed as he and his companions followed the man into the big house.

The front hall, covered with a black-and-white tile floor in a checkerboard pattern, was enormous. It extended to a ballroom where dozens of men and women in formal dress danced, drank and conversed. Servants clad in red jackets carried trays of food and drinks among the guests. Patches of cigar smoke drifted above a group of men at a far corner of the room, standing apart from the others.

The Phoenix trio did not get a chance to see the ballroom in more detail. The bodyguard hastily escorted them into a cloakroom, followed by two more servants in red. They could have all been former professional football players. It appeared that de Madrid hired servants based on their muscle bulk and the grimness of their features.

"I'm sorry, gentlemen," the bodyguard who had spoken to them earlier said, "but we have been instructed to search you before we allow you to enter the main ballroom. It is a matter of security. I hope you understand."

"Of course," Katz said with a nod. "Mr. de Madrid does not know us and he must be careful. Trust is something one must earn. *Oui?*"

"I'm glad you understand," the guard replied.

"I understand," Katz assured him, "but I must make certain my associates also comprehend this situation so we do not have any unnecessary unpleasantness. *N'est-ce pas?*"

"By all means," the man agreed.

Katz addressed James and Manning in rapid French. Both men nodded and slowly unbuttoned their jackets. They removed the garments to reveal shoulder holsters with .38 revolvers sheathed in leather under their arms, then calmly allowed the handguns to be confiscated by the guards.

"We will return these guns to you when you leave," the guy in charge assured them. "Do you carry any other weapons?"

"No," Katz answered, gesturing with the gloved hand of his prosthesis. "But continue the search if you wish."

They did. De Madrid's men patted down the Phoenix Force trio, checking for ankle holsters, forearm sheaths, weapons at the small of the back or concealed in pockets. They were also checking for "wires," hidden microphones carried by undercover cops to record conversations for evidence. The servants were very thorough and examined buttons, shoes and creases in clothing with suspicion.

Katz's artificial arm surprised the guards. They seemed almost embarrassed as they examined the limb to make certain it was genuine. The contraption of plastic and steel strapped to the stump of the Israeli's right arm was not the sort of thing they were accustomed to handling. None of them really wanted to touch it. Like many people, the servants were uncomfortable in the presence of an amputee.

"Bone cancer," Katz explained. In fact, he had lost his arm in an explosion during the Six-Day War in the Middle East more than twenty years before.

"I'm sorry, Mr. Picard," the bodyguard said awkwardly.

*"Il n'y a pas de quoi,"* Katz said with a shrug. "It is no problem. *Oui?"*

The bodyguards nodded. They did not suspect that the index finger of the gloved "hand" was actually the barrel of a .22 Magnum built into Katz's prosthesis. Nor did they guess that a high-frequency radio-microphone had been installed inside the artificial limb.

"I feel I should introduce myself," the leader of the servants began. "My name is Jemal. I apologize for this inconvenience and shall now take you to see Mr. de Madrid."

The three Phoenix Force commandos followed Jemal from the cloakroom into the hall. He led them past most of the guests in the ballroom. Couples danced to the music of the famous *Blue Danube* waltz by Strauss, performed by a band of orchestra musicians hired for the event. Some of the guests were content to drink champagne or stuff themselves at the buffet table. A few were bent over a mirror decorated with lines of white powder, snorting cocaine into their nostrils with glass straws.

Something for everybody, James thought as he glanced around at the regal setting. In addition to the wine and coke, high-priced ladies of the evening made certain none of the male guests were lonely. Middle-aged men sat with the expensive call girls, counting out cash while the females encouraged their generosity by displaying phony smiles and fondling the men suggestively.

Jemal escorted the Phoenix trio to a patio outside the hacienda. There were party-goers here as well, splashing in a kidney-shaped swimming pool. Some had not bothered to wear a bathing suit or trunks: a few were in their underwear, and others swam nude.

A group of men standing in a circle around a pit in the back lawn, despite their elegant attire in tuxedos and white dinner jackets, cheered and shouted in the style of men at a boxing match. They sounded like the types who enjoyed the violence of the sport without any appreciation of the skill. Jemal led James, Katz and Manning to the jeering spectators.

The sound of snarling animals revealed that the group was watching a sick, sadistic sport: two pit bulldogs tearing each other apart. Money was exchanged as the spectators bet on which poor beast would be the victor.

"Just a moment, gentlemen," Jemal urged as they waited for the snarls to end.

Soon only one dog growled. The other whimpered helplessly until a loud crunch of bone announced that its neck had been crushed by the jaws of its opponent. Several men cheered, and others moaned with disappointment. Losers paid the winners.

The three men of Phoenix Force were disgusted by the exhibition. None had any desire to watch the brutal entertainment that had been staged for the group of bastards. It wasn't that the men of Phoenix Force were squeamish. They had seen destruction a thousand times; each of them had lost count of how many opponents he had killed. But they had never murdered for pleasure or without good reason. Forcing two animals to fight to the death for the enjoyment of spectators was part of the worst side of man's makeup. The side that should have been left behind in the caves when human beings had started to walk up-right.

"Hello," said a short, fat man with a round, dark face capped by a wavy mop of black hair, obviously a toupee, as he approached the three Phoenix fighters. "I am Gabriel Carlos de Madrid. Welcome to my home."

"Hello," Katz replied. He turned toward Manning and James. "I am Henri Picard from the Pointe Basse Trust and Investment Foundation. These are my associates, Mr. Bellefontaine and Mr. Maarten."

"A pleasure to meet you," de Madrid declared, smiling and bobbing his head like a toy dog ornament in the back window of a moving car. "Of course, I realize you are actually here to speak to one of my guests. A man whom I have often done business with and known for many years."

"That's what we've heard, Mr. de Madrid," Katz replied.

"Please." The plantation owner raised his hands and waved urgently. "Call me Carlos, *s'il vous plaît*. We're going to have another dogfight as soon as they clean up the mess down in the pit. Care to make a bet?"

"We're bankers, not gamblers," Katz told him.

"Bankers gamble all the time," Montgomery Penn stated as he joined the discussion. "Beautiful system you've got, too. You only gamble with money that belongs to somebody else. That way you never lose, eh?"

"Bankers have gone to jail for that sort of attitude, Mr. Penn," Katz declared, gazing into the grinning face of the mulatto gangster. "You are Mr. Penn?"

"Actually," Penn began, lighting a Turkish cigarette with his gold-plated lighter, "I'm using a different name tonight. Let's talk over by the trees. You don't mind missin' the dogfight, do you?"

"We can live with the disappointment," Manning told him, a trace of French accent in his voice and an undisguised and genuine contempt for the cruel and bloodthirsty form of entertainment.

"You don't do this sort of thing in Martinique, eh?" Penn laughed. "How about boxing? You look big enough to hold your own in the ring. That is, if you got any guts and you know how to use your fists."

"I'm just a bank security officer and adviser, *monsieur*," Manning replied. "I never claimed to be a pugilist."

"Jemal told Carlos two of you blokes were packin' guns," Penn remarked as he escorted the Phoenix trio toward a row of coconut-palm trees. "Guess you don't need to box when you got a gun."

"These matters have nothing to do with business," Katz complained. "We were told you are interested in investing money in a special confidential account in Martinique."

"True," Penn nodded. "I'm just surprised little Kevinson got contacts like you. That is, if you really are bankers from Martinique."

Two figures approached them. One man was heavily muscled and looked like a professional wrestler dressed in a tuxedo. The other man was tall and slender and moved with a feline grace. Carrying a swagger stick with a silver handle, he seemed to glide across the lawn, and a black top hat was perched on his head.

Holy hell, Calvin James thought as he recognized the familiar figure of a living nightmare that he had thought had ended years ago. It's Cercueil!

His skin crawled when he saw the incarnation of a man he had killed long ago. A human monster who had been the mastermind of the Black Alchemists. A cunning and cold-blooded butcher with less regard for human life than a hungry vulture.

The sight of the new Cercueil, with his undertaker's hat and death's-head walking stick, startled Katz and Manning nearly as badly as it had James. Hadn't the badass from Chicago personally killed the first Cercueil in the Colorado headquarters of the infamous Black Alchemists? James was unable to remove his eyes from the sinister figure.

He knew it couldn't be Maurice Cercueil. That was impossible. The Ton Ton Macoute chief wasn't really a *bocor* who could summon the spirits of voodoo and Baron Samedi back from the dead.

But James had to be sure. He had to know for certain he wasn't seeing the same man he had decapitated four years ago.

"Who are they?" Katz asked Penn, turning to face the Jamaican gangster and tilting his head toward the Haitians. "The local chimney sweeps?"

*"Bon soir,"* Cercueil greeted them with a smile as cold as a grinning skull. *"Comment allez-vous?"*

*"Très bien,"* Katz replied with a nod. *"Merci, monsieur. Et vous?"*

*"Bien, bien,"* Cercueil answered. He continued to address the three Phoenix commandos in French. "You gentlemen are from Martinique?"

"Perhaps," Katz said, raising an eyebrow. "Who are you, *monsieur*, and what do you want with us?"

"Who I am is not important," the Haitian replied, toying with his swagger stick. He glanced at Calvin James, who was still staring at him. "Your accent sounds more European than Martiniquais."

"I am from France," Katz said. "Are you a policeman? You wish to see my passport?"

"No need," Cercueil assured him, fixing his gaze on Calvin James. "Is there a reason I fascinate you so, Monsieur—?"

"Bellefontaine," James answered. "I did not stare at you on purpose, but I haven't seen anyone dressed like Fred Astaire for a long time. Is there a special reason for that outfit?"

"Watch your tongue or you might lose it," Louis de Broglie warned. The big, muscular Haitian glared at James and folded thick arms on his barrel chest.

"Louis," Cercueil shook his head. "Don't take offense at Monsieur Bellefontaine's remark. It is just the sort of stupid thing Americans say when they don't understand something."

James stiffened. He felt his stomach knot as Cercueil fixed his icy gaze on the Phoenix pro's face. A smug smile slithered across the Haitian's lips.

"Your French is fluent, Bellefontaine—although I doubt that is your true name," Cercueil began, switching to English. "But your accent is less than perfect. You are from the United States. The Midwest, perhaps?"

"Born and raised in Chicago," James admitted. "Got in a little trouble back there a few years ago and moved to Martinique for my health."

"Your health?" The Haitian raised his eyebrows.

"The idea of going to prison makes me break out in a rash," James said with a shrug.

"Hey," Montgomery Penn snapped, opening his jacket in case he needed to draw his Largo pistol from shoulder leather. "What the fuck is this? You blokes are suppose to be from Martinique—"

"We are from Martinique," Katz told him. "You think everyone who lives on that island was born there? *Zut alors!* What sort of games are you playing here? Kevinson said we'd be dealing with you, not these Haitians."

"Why do you think we're Haitians?" Cercueil inquired.

"You aren't the only person who can recognize a regional accent," the Israeli replied. "My bank did business with some of your government officials before Duvalier's government fell. You people were never a very good risk."

"That might change," Cercueil replied. "*Excusez-moi*, but I simply tested you gentlemen to see if you really are from Martinique. At least you speak French.

Unfortunately, I'm still not certain about you one way or the other."

"Mr. Penn," Manning said with a sigh. "Are we going to discuss the possibility of opening a confidential account at our bank, or do we spend the rest of the evening with this idiotic chatter?"

"Please, let's discuss business," Cercueil urged. "You don't mind if I chat with Mr. Bellefontaine for a moment?"

"Just don't wander out of sight," Katz replied. "I like to know where my men are."

"Of course," the Haitian agreed. He turned to James. "No objections to a little private conversation? I'm curious about the opinions of an American."

"Sure," James agreed, but his skin crawled as he followed Cercueil. Although it wasn't the same man he had killed in Colorado, there was a remarkable similarity to the original Cercueil. Deceptively charming, clever and dangerous.

The Haitian led James away from the others and to a small wooden bridge that extended across a thin stream of water between two miniature ponds. Frogs croaked softly as moonlight reflected on the surface of the water.

"You left America because you were in trouble with the law," Cercueil mused, staring at the white globe that shimmered on the pond surface as if it were a crystal ball. "Why did you go to Martinique? Because you speak French?"

"Seemed like a good reason," James answered.

"Why didn't you come to Haiti instead?" Cercueil asked.

"Gimme a break," James snorted. "Haiti has the lowest standard of living in the Western Hemisphere."

"Many American tourists don't find that so bad," the Haitian remarked. "They like to fish and stay at the hotels in Port-au-Prince. Some enjoy the casinos."

"I needed a place to live, not a vacation spot," James stated. "Don't tell me you're upset that I didn't want to live in Haiti. If it's so great, how come you're here?"

"I have my reasons," Cercueil replied. "At least Haiti was an independent nation."

*"Was?"* James inquired. "Thought it still is. Just 'cause Baby Doc has gone doesn't mean it has become a puppet government to anybody else."

"It isn't a country anymore," Cercueil said sadly. "It is just a maelstrom of chaos and anarchy without law and order or control. Yet it was a nation of black people ruled by a *black* president. Martinique is a slave state where blacks are subject to the white government of France. Just as in America, where you were a black peasant to a white-dominated power structure."

"Sure," James chuckled. "I could've gone to Haiti and maybe lived in a chicken coop instead. Maybe I'd be lucky and the Ton Ton Macoute would decide not to use it for target practice, huh?"

"Really?" Cercueil glared at James and gripped his swagger stick in both fists.

The Phoenix pro felt a cold tremor shift up his spine. The first Cercueil had carried a walking stick very similar to the one the Haitian held. It was a cane sword with a long, razor-sharp blade sheathed in its wooden shaft. James wondered if such a weapon was also hidden in the new Cercueil's swagger stick.

"Do most black Americans share your opinion of Haiti under the rule of Duvalier and his son?" Cercueil asked. "Do they also feel contempt and loathing for the Ton Ton Macoute?"

"I don't think most Americans—black or white—paid much attention to Haiti until Jean-Claude split," James answered. "Kind of odd, when you think about it. You see, in the United States a lot of people are protesting apartheid in South Africa because blacks don't get equal treatment in that country. Before that they protested the white government of Rhodesia for the same reason. Yet blacks had virtually no human rights in Haiti—except the government bosses and the Ton Ton Macoute, of course. Hardly anyone in America seemed to give a damn. Maybe if Duvalier had been white or a Communist or whatever it would have been different. I guess most people figured a black dictator with black storm troopers could do whatever he wanted to black people in his own country."

"So you hated the Duvaliers and the Ton Ton Macoute?" Cercueil said softly, a slight edge to his tone, like a razor resting on velvet.

"I don't like tyrants and I don't like police states," James admitted. "You expect me to figure it's okay that a black ruler and his homegrown Gestapo can prove they're as bad as any of their white counterparts in other countries? That's one form of equality I can do without. The whole fucking world can do without it."

"Well..." Cercueil's smile seemed frozen in a jack-o'-lantern grin as he spoke through clenched teeth. "I did ask your opinion, didn't I? Shall we see how the others are doing, Mr. Bellefontaine?"

## 10

"What have we got so far?" Rafael Encizo asked as he entered the special surveillance van parked by the wire mesh fence at the end of the sugarcane fields.

"They made contact with Penn," Rodney Leaky replied. The small, wiry black man sat on a folding chair beside a wall of radio receivers, tape recorders and night-sight scanning gear. A headset was clamped around his skull, and the reels of a large recorder turned steadily. "Good idea your mate had about putting that radio mike in his artificial arm. Never thought of a trick like that, and I've been doin' this sort of thing for eight years."

Leaky was an expert in electronic surveillance. He was a professional snoop, an eavesdropping expert from the governor-general's council on internal security. Colonel Wells had assured them little Rodney was the best man for the job. So far, Leaky had lived up to the colonel's claim.

"What have they been talking about in there?" the Cuban commando inquired as he unbuttoned the high collar of his chauffeur's uniform. "Anything we can nail them on?"

"Not much so far," Leaky admitted, polishing the thick lenses of his wire-rimmed glasses. "Penn has discussed his desire for a confidential bank account, but he seems reluctant to trust your friends. Some Haitians were talking to them in French, and I don't know what that was about—"

Encizo cut him off. "Haitians? Are you sure they're Haitians?"

"That's what they said," Leaky confirmed. "Why would anybody lie about being Haitian?"

"Stay on it," Encizo urged as he grabbed his Heckler & Koch MP-5 from a weapons rack and bolted out the door.

Outside, David McCarter nervously paced the muddy ground, splattering his paratrooper boots as he muttered to himself. McCarter was all dressed up for combat, clad in black night camouflage uniform. An Ingram M-10 machine pistol hung from a shoulder strap near his right hip, and a Browning Hi-Power autoloader pistol was tucked in shoulder leather under his left arm. Spare ammo magazines for both weapons were stored in belt pouches. He even carried an SAS flash-bang concussion grenade. McCarter was ready for a fight and champing at the bit to get on with it.

"They pulled a surprise on us, David," Encizo said softly. "There are Haitians at Señor de Madrid's little party."

"Bloody hell," McCarter rasped. "Cercueil one of 'em?"

"I wouldn't be surprised," the Cuban answered. "Whoever they are, they seem to be chummy with Penn."

"We might have a chance to get all the ringleaders at once," McCarter said eagerly. "I say we raid the bloody party. Grab Cercueil, Penn and maybe a couple of others."

"What are we gonna charge them with?" Encizo asked.

"Who cares?" the Briton snorted. "Let's just get them and let Calvin pump some scopolamine in the bastards. After they talk, we'll be able to get all the evidence we need to shut them down for good."

"That's blunt, crude and impulsive," Encizo remarked. "Not to mention illegal as hell."

"So is terrorism," McCarter insisted. "You know my plans are never very fancy, but they usually work."

"Let's wait a bit," Encizo urged. "Maybe Rodney will get some more evidence on tape so the Jamaicans will be able to put the terrorists behind bars without having to ignore every right granted to their people under their constitution."

"Regardless of what else happens," McCarter said, "we have to get our hands on Cercueil. If he gets away, this whole mess will just start up again somewhere else."

"You two seem to be having an intense conversation," Sergeant Bristol remarked as he stepped from the cab of the surveillance van. "What is it? Or can't I be trusted with the details?"

Bristol was bitter because he felt his own department was trying to burn him for shooting a suspect in the back. He was not happy to be part of the backup team with Encizo and McCarter. Although this suggested he was still needed for the mission, Bristol felt he had been placed in the least important role as driver of the van because they did not trust him with anything more complex.

He also resented having to take orders from the foreigners, especially McCarter. Bristol's unreasonable hatred of Britons made the task even more unpleasant for the Kingston cop. Not unlike most bigots, Bristol tended to put as much blame as possible on the nationality he was prejudiced against. Everything that was wrong with Jamaica just had to be the fault of the British who had formerly ruled the island nation, along with any Brits who still lived in Jamaica. Working with an actual British citizen—a white man with an East London accent—was the ultimate humiliation for Bristol.

"We're trying to decide on strategy—" Encizo began, but he abruptly went silent as a pair of headlights cut through the darkness.

An American-made army-surplus jeep approached the van along the muddied track; a grim-faced driver sat behind the steering wheel while another figure stood up, pointing a British Sterling submachine gun over the top of the windshield at McCarter, Encizo and Bristol. The jeep rolled to a halt, headlights trained on the two Phoenix fighters and their Jamaican ally.

"This is private property," the man with the chattergun declared. "You're bloody well trespassin'."

"Kingston police," Bristol replied, reaching for his badge folder. "Put down that gun or—"

Encizo suddenly slammed into Bristol, knocking him off his feet, driving him to the ground. The cop and the Cuban fell just as a burst of 9 mm rounds snarled from the gunman's Sterling, raking the side of the van. Rodney Leaky cried out, but his voice was distorted by the sound of gunshots. The others did not know if the CIS snoop had been injured or merely frightened.

McCarter had dropped to one knee, grabbed his Ingram and immediately returned fire. He triggered a long salvo of parabellum slugs that ripped into the upper torso of the enemy gunman, who tumbled sideways over the edge of the jeep, downed by the force of five 115-grain bullets.

Encizo adopted a prone stance, holding the H&K submachine gun in both hands as he aimed the muzzle at the jeep's windshield. The driver, who had ducked during the shooting, now raised his head with a pistol in one fist. Encizo fired a 3-round volley. A trio of bullet holes cracked a spiderweb pattern in the glass, and the driver's face was transformed into a crimson smear.

"Rodney!" McCarter shouted as he ran to the rear of the van. "You all right, Rodney?"

"I...I think so," the electronic snoop replied in an unsteady voice as he staggered from the vehicle. The wire-rimmed glasses hung crookedly on his nose, and his hands were still shaking. "A couple bullets pierced the wall. I think one took out the radio."

"You can't just gun down people in cold blood," Bristol snapped, looking for someone to lash out at and choosing McCarter as the best choice. "We're supposed to represent law and order."

"That bloke fired his weapon first," the Briton told him. "Besides, I'm not a bleedin' copper. You want to get killed in the line of duty, that's your business, but don't expect me to join you."

"Why don't you two save this for later?" Encizo advised, staring at the fields of sugarcane in the soggy ground beyond the fence. "I wonder if they heard the shooting at the hacienda."

"Depends on how loud the party is," McCarter commented. "If de Madrid has more than one security patrol roving about, the shots were probably heard by the others. Maybe we'll be lucky and the rest of the guards will be hangin' around the house, watchin' the guests."

"We'd better not count on being lucky," Encizo said, sliding the strap of his MP-5 onto his shoulder. "Carver and I are gonna take the limo and head around front. It will seem less suspicious than the van. You guys radio for help."

"I suggest you blokes don't hang around here while you're waiting," McCarter added. "More of de Madrid's men might show up."

"Good idea," Leaky said, bobbing his head as if trying to work it loose from his neck. He was accustomed to radios and telescopes, not guns and bullets.

# PULL THE PIN ON ADVENTURE,

... get 4 explosive novels
plus a pocketknife

# FREE

# Score a direct hit by accepting our dynamite free offer

Here's a no-holds-barred, free-for-all chance for you to blast your way through the hottest action-adventure novels ever published.

Just return the attached card, and we'll send you 4 gut-chilling, high-voltage novels just like the one you're reading— plus a versatile pocketknife— ABSOLUTELY FREE!

They're yours to keep even if you never buy another Gold Eagle novel. But we're betting you'll want to join the legion of fans who get Gold Eagle books delivered right to their home on a regular basis. Here's why. . .

## 7 GREAT REASONS TO BECOME A SUBSCRIBER:

As a Gold Eagle subscriber, you'll get: • 6 new titles every other month • 11% savings off retail prices—you pay only $2.49 per book plus 95¢ postage and handling per shipment • books hot off the presses and before they're available at retail stores • delivery right to your home • FREE newsletter with every shipment • always the right to cancel and owe nothing • eligibility to receive special books at deep discount prices

The grenade's in your hand. Go for it!

This offer is too good to miss . . .
RUSH YOUR ORDER TO US TODAY

## Yours free—this stainless-steel pocketknife

Talk about versatile! You get 7 functions in this one handy device—screwdriver, bottle opener, nail cleaner, nail file, knife, scissors and key chain. Perfect for pocket, tool kit, tackle box. And it's yours free when you return this card.

FREE

Peel off grenade from front cover and slam it down here

# PULL THE PIN ON ADVENTURE

## Rush my 4 free books and my free pocketknife.

Then send me 6 brand-new Gold Eagle novels (2 *Mack Bolans* and one each of *Able Team*, *Phoenix Force*, *Vietnam: Ground Zero* and *SOBs*) every second month as outlined on the opposite page. I understand I am under no obligation to purchase any books.

166 CIM PAMW

Name _____ (PLEASE PRINT)

Address _____ Apt. No. _____

City _____ State _____ Zip Code _____

This offer is limited to one order per household and not valid to present subscribers. Price is subject to change.

## The most pulse-pounding, pressure-packed action reading ever published

Razor-edge storytelling. Page-crackling tension. On-target firepower. Hard-punching excitement. Gold Eagle books slam home raw action the way you like it—hard, fast and real!

If offer card below is missing, write to Gold Eagle Reader Service, 901 Fuhrmann Blvd., P.O. Box 1867, Buffalo, NY 14269-1867

"You go ahead," Bristol declared. He glared at McCarter and Encizo. "I'm going with you two."

"We can cover each other," Encizo told him. "Rodney might need your help if he gets in trouble before reinforcements arrive."

"You mean you don't trust me," Bristol muttered.

"We don't have time to worry about whether you like it or not," McCarter said gruffly. "We told you what to do and you'll damn well do it. The success of this mission is more important than your opinion of us, Bristol."

"So are the lives of our partners," Encizo added. "Which may be in jeopardy right now."

MOST OF THE GUESTS at the Palace of Madrid failed to notice the distant chatter of automatic weapons that drifted across the sugarcane crop. Another dogfight was in progress in the pit, and de Madrid and several of his guests were cheering on the beasts. The waltz music inside the house had been replaced with a loud rock-and-roll number featuring lots of amplified electric guitar, thundering drums and a female vocalist who seemed to do more screaming and howling than singing.

However, Katz, James and Manning recognized the familiar sound of automatic fire and guessed that it meant McCarter and Encizo had encountered opposition. Cercueil and Montgomery Penn also heard the shooting. Penn suddenly lost interest in discussing banking practices in Martinique. He left the three

Phoenix Force commandos and headed for the dog-pit to speak with de Madrid.

Cercueil and Louis de Broglie remained with the Phoenix trio. The two Haitians had drawn pistols from their jackets and pointed them at the "bankers" from Martinique.

"Don't call out or do anything to draw attention," Cercueil instructed, aiming a silver-plated .25 auto at Katz's stomach. "Don't raise your hands, but keep them where we can see them."

"We were already searched before we came in," the Israeli stated, holding the gloved hand of his prosthesis in his left palm. "What is this for?"

"You gentlemen suddenly arrive here after a rushed invitation arranged by an associate of Mr. Penn," the Haitian replied. "Now someone is firing full-auto weapons somewhere on the plantation. I'm very suspicious of coincidence. I don't believe your presence here isn't connected with the shooting...any more than I believe you three are bankers from Martinique."

"So you figure we're cops or something?" James asked, glancing at the snubnose .357 Magnum in de Broglie's big fist. "Stuff it, man. This isn't Haiti under your hero Papa Doc. You can't expect to kill people in front of dozens of witnesses and just walk away."

"Shut up," de Broglie grunted, cocking the hammer of his revolver to emphasize the order.

"You'd better listen to Bellefontaine instead of thinking like a Ton Ton Macoute storm trooper,"

Gary Manning stated. "If the police are out there, you ought to be concerned with getting away from here. They're probably after Penn, not you two. Maybe de Madrid is the main target. They have enough cocaine in there to get an elephant high for a week. If you leave now, you can probably get away...."

"How considerate," Cercueil said with a smile. "I don't know who you are, but I don't believe you're bankers. I've met a number of bankers from the Antilles Islands before. They talk more than they listen. They chatter about what a wonderful system of savings and investment their bank offers, and they generally warn that these golden opportunities won't last long and urge their potential clients to act quickly. You didn't act that way. You seemed too curious about Penn's activities and associates and not the least concerned about the interests of your bank. Whatever you are, you aren't bankers."

Penn approached the Haitians while de Madrid began hustling his guests into the house. Jemal and two other servants in red jackets walked toward the three Phoenix Force captives. Katz wondered how much longer they could stall the outlaws. Long enough for the others to come to their assistance?

Calvin James figured the odds on taking on the captors without the cavalry arriving to bail them out. Hell, he thought, McCarter, Encizo and the others might have their hands full with de Madrid's security people. From the way Penn seemed to be giving orders to Jemal and the other "help," James suspected those guys were probably Jamaican gunsels on Penn's payroll. A thug dressed up in a fancy suit was still a thug.

The odds didn't look very good. Cercueil and his muscle-bound Haitian pal were armed, and both were smart enough to stay eight or nine feet away, far enough that it was futile for James to try to grab an opponent's gun hand or to kick the weapon out of his grasp. Penn and his hired hoods were no doubt armed, as well. Three against six—not including the other goons prowling around the estate. Except for Katz's single-shot .22 Magnum, all the guns were in the hands of the enemy. Poor odds, but as long as the three Phoenix warriors were still alive, they had a chance.

"Penn," Cercueil began, not taking his eyes from Katz or altering the aim of his little silver pistol. "These so-called bankers are here because of you. This is your dirty laundry, and you're the one who'll take care of it."

"Goddamn it, Cercueil," the Jamaican gangster complained, drawing a Largo pistol from his jacket. "These blokes could be genuine. In fact, we don't have any proof otherwise."

"Get rid of them," Cercueil ordered as he stepped back and slipped his .25 auto into a pocket. "Have de Madrid help you with the bodies. Whatever you do, you'd better do it fast."

Cercueil and de Broglie turned to leave. Penn opened his mouth but decided any protest was useless. Jemal and his two comrades had also drawn weapons and pointed the guns at the three Phoenix Force pros.

"You two really are Ton Ton Macoute," Gary Manning jeered at the Haitians' backs. "Shooting unarmed peasants for sport is your style, but when people start to fight back, you're ready to run."

Louis de Broglie spun about, his eyes blazing with anger. The big Haitian stepped forward and swung a wild right cross at Manning's head. The Canadian warrior weaved slightly to avoid the full impact of the other man's knuckles. The punch still connected, but it appeared to have more force than the blow actually delivered. Manning's head snapped back and he fell ungracefully to the ground.

"You don't fight so good, white pig," de Broglie growled as he swung a leather-shod foot into Manning's stomach. "I like to beat up whitey pigs. Like to kill them!"

He kicked Manning in the ribs. The Canadian groaned loudly and curled into a ball on the ground. He began coughing as if he might throw up and moaned, "No, no..."

"Come, Louis," Cercueil ordered sharply. "There isn't time for this."

"Fishbelly-pale lump of shit," the big Haitian growled, and spat on Manning's bowed head.

*"Au revoir,"* Cercueil announced, throwing off a mocking salute with a gesture of the death's-head handle of his walking stick. "It has been interesting. Too bad, Mr. Bellefontaine. It appears you should have gone to Haiti after all."

"Maybe you shouldn't have left," James replied, sounding a hell of a lot more confident than he felt. "We'll talk about it next time, fella."

"I doubt that," Cercueil said with amusement. He hoisted the cane across his shoulder and headed for the house, followed by Louis de Broglie.

Glancing over his shoulder at the two Haitians, Penn muttered something. The gangster aimed his Largo pistol at James while Jemal covered Katz. The other two henchmen, each holding a snubnose revolver, seemed uncertain of what to do. Gary Manning was still curled in a ball on the ground, hugging his belly, moaning softly.

"What are we going to do with these fellers, Mr. Penn?" Jemal inquired.

"There's got to be somewhere to dispose of three bodies around here," Penn replied gruffly. "Doesn't Carlos have a big furnace somewhere in the fields? Sort of an incinerator to burn up waste products left over from chopping the sugarcane?"

"I think so," the henchman answered, "but I really don't know any more than you do about how this plantation is set up."

"Shit," Penn rasped through his teeth. "We'll have to get Carlos. This is his bloody problem, too."

"We're not goin' into them fields, mon," Jemal said, glaring at his boss. "A bunch of those things are out there—"

"Don't talk like one of those idiots from the obeah cults," Penn snapped. "We got more cause to be worried 'bout the coppers than those brain-dead bastards.''

Manning started to rise and moaned loudly. Then he fell on his side, still clutching his ribs. Penn clucked his tongue in disgust.

"He . . . broke . . . my ribs," Manning groaned.

"Christ," Penn muttered. He turned to his flunkies. "Get this overgrown sissy to his feet."

Jemal, his gun still trained on Katz, jerked his head toward Manning. The two underlings nodded and stepped toward the groaning Canadian. They jammed the guns into their belts, then dragged Manning to his feet.

"Get up, ya paleface weaklin'," one man growled as he grabbed Manning's left wrist and pulled.

Gary Manning sprung from the ground like a rocket. His right fist smashed into the point of the thug's chin with bone-jarring force and precision. The punch lifted the startled hood off his feet to land abruptly on his ass. The second goon gasped with surprise and reached for the Magnum in his belt.

The Canadian snap-kicked the guy in the groin. The polished tip of his shoe caught the thug in the testicles. He uttered a bestial moan of pain and folded at the middle. The hood managed to draw his revolver, but Manning's fist delivered a hammerlike blow to the man's arm. The gun fell from shaky fingers, and Manning's other fist slammed into the thug's jaw to knock him to the ground.

Startled by the scuffle, Jemal turned. Katz had been waiting for such an opportunity. From the moment

Manning had provoked de Broglie, Katz had known that the clever Canadian was setting a trap for their opponents. Manning's trick had distracted the enemy, and Katz quickly took advantage of it.

The Phoenix Force commander pointed the gloved index finger of his prosthetic arm at Jemal's head. Katz flexed the muscles in the stump of his abbreviated arm to trigger the built-in gun. The crack of the high-velocity projectile sang into the night as flame appeared from the end of the "finger." Jemal never heard the shot. Moving faster than sound, the diminutive .22 bullet punched a hole through Jemal's skull between the left eyebrow and temple. The slug burned into his brain and tore an exit at the back of his head.

Calvin James also took advantage of the distraction arranged by Gary Manning. When Montgomery Penn turned toward the fistfight, James delivered a sword-kick. The edge of his shoe chopped into the back of Penn's wrist, and the Largo pistol dropped to the floor.

"Wha—?" Penn gasped as James followed through with an uppercut to his stomach.

Intending to deliver a karate chop to the side of Penn's neck with his other hand, James missed his target and smacked the gangster's right ear instead. Penn staggered backward from the blow but did not go down. The Jamaican crime boss had not become a big fish in a violent world without being plenty tough.

He jammed a solid right into James's sternum. The Chicago-bred commando grunted from the pain of the blow but managed to fully dodge the left hook Penn swung next. James lashed out another fast tae kwon-do kick and drove his shoe under Penn's rib cage.

The gangster moaned as James moved behind him and rammed a *seiken* punch to his opponent's kidney. The Phoenix fighter did not let up. He slammed a karate chop between the guy's shoulder blades, then grabbed Penn's jacket collar. He yanked hard and kicked Penn's feet out from under him. The gangster fell on his back hard, the wind knocked out of him.

Manning had decked both of his opponents, but now one slowly rose and reached for his .357. Manning's fist connected with the guy's head; as the hoodlum started to fall, the Canadian knocked the gun from his belt with one hand and grabbed the lapel of the goon's fancy red jacket with the other.

Twisting the cloth, Manning shoved the guy upward. His other hand snaked between the hoodlum's thighs. The man cried out as Manning scooped him up in a crotch-lift. The powerful Canadian raised the hapless hood over his head, turned him upside down and hurled him at the second opponent who was just rising to his feet.

The human projectile slammed the other man to the ground. Both moaned, dizzy and dazed. Manning quickly scooped up the hoodlums' revolvers, holding a .357 in each fist. Glancing around, he noticed James and Katz had likewise taken care of Penn and Jemal and confiscated their opponents' 9 mm pistols.

"Oh, God!" a voice cried out.

Gabriel Carlos de Madrid and three hoods in red jackets had returned from the great house. The rich man waved a chrome-plated .45 Government Colt. Two of his companions carried handguns. The third held a Stirling submachine gun.

Yakov Katzenelenbogen reacted first, instinctively aiming his gun at the opponent who presented the greatest threat. He pressed his thumb on the safety catch to be certain the unfamiliar Largo pistol was ready to fire. Then he squeezed the trigger. Two 9 mm shots bored into the chest of the guy with the Sterling blast machine. The gunner screamed and went down without firing the British chattergun.

One of the red-jacketed gunmen swung his Smith & Wesson revolver toward Katz. Calvin James, holding the Largo pistol taken from Penn, snap-aimed the weapon at the gunman who was about to waste Katz. James fired hastily and hit the gunsel in the upper arm. The force of the slug spun the guy around as James triggered two more shots. One bullet tore into the man's breastbone, shattering the sternal notch. The other 9 mm ripped through the hoodlum's heart.

Carlos de Madrid fired a panic-stricken shot at the Phoenix trio. He didn't bother to aim his Colt auto-loader, perhaps expecting fate to guide his bullet. Fate did not. The big .45 slug tore into the ground between James and Katz. De Madrid's arm jerked violently upward with the recoil. The plantation owner had owned the gun for years, but this was the first time he had ever fired it. De Madrid discovered too late that just owning a gun did not mean one knew how to use it.

Manning fired one of the two Magnum revolvers taken from his vanquished opponents. The powerful snubgun bucked in his fist. The third bodyguard with de Madrid shrieked as a 158-grain .357 projectile sliced through his belly. The high-velocity slug ravaged his intestines and ripped through his left kidney. The man collapsed, blood seeping from his bullet-gouged body.

The Magnum in Manning's left fist roared a split second later. A second slug slammed into de Madrid's left leg. The shot was poorly aimed and almost missed the plantation owner. The powerful Magnum round ripped into de Madrid's thigh, plowing through flesh and muscle. The bullet missed the bone but caused massive tissue damage as it penetrated de Madrid's leg with brain-numbing force.

The man whirled, fell, and tumbled several feet to the edge of the pit. The wild snarling and snapping sounds of battling pit bulls still emanated from the trench. De Madrid screamed as he slid over the edge. He released his Colt .45 to cling desperately to the lip of the pit into which his legs and lower torso dangerously dangled.

"Help me!" de Madrid cried as he clawed at the concrete to try to pull himself up.

He shrieked as the dogs turned on the intruder. De Madrid's fingers scraped the edge of the pit, then vanished from view. The snarling of the pit bulls accompanied de Madrid's screams. The man who had enjoyed watching the vicious dogfights was now a participant.

"Jesus," Calvin James rasped. "Those dogs will tear him to pieces."

"Yeah," Manning commented, unable to feel much sympathy for a man who mistreated animals in such a fashion. "Isn't that a shame?"

"Penn!" Katz shouted, pointing his Largo pistol at the retreating figure of the Jamaican gangster, who had dashed for the house while the three Phoenix commandos were busy with de Madrid and his gunsels. Before Katz could get a clear target, the crime boss ducked through the French doors and vanished from view. However, another figure appeared at the threshold—holding an FMK-3 submachine gun, an Argentine weapon similar in design to an Uzi.

The three Phoenix pros instantly dropped to the ground and ducked behind some palm trees as the FMK-3 blasted a ruthless volley of 9 mm rounds. Bullets splintered chunks of bark from the tree trunks, but none struck the trio of warriors. Dirt spit up from the ground near Manning's left leg as a ricochet struck the earth beside him.

"Cover me!" James called out as he leaned around the tree shielding him and fired at the French doors.

The bullets whined against the frame of the doorway and convinced the gunman to stay behind cover. James took a deep breath and ran for the doors, head low, back arched, pistol held in a two-handed grip, arms extended and elbows slightly bent.

As the FMK-3 gunner poked the stubby barrel of his weapon through the doorway, Katz and Manning opened fire, careful to avoid hitting James as the black commando dashed toward the house. Bullets pelted the doorway and drove the machine gunner back.

Closing in, James dived to the patio, hitting the pavement in a fast shoulder roll. Pain laced a bruised deltoid muscle as he completed the motion and landed in a kneeling stance near the French doors, pistol aimed at the threshold. The guy with the FMK-3 leaned around the corner to fire his Argentinian blaster.

Calvin James fired his Largo twice. One bullet drilled the gunman under the rib cage; the other pierced the solar plexus and tore upward into his heart. The man dropped his submachine gun and slumped to the floor. He was very, very dead.

James glanced inside the house, standing clear of the doors in case more armed opponents lurked inside. The ballroom was a mess. Furniture had been bowled over by the fleeing guests. The floor was covered in dropped food, spilled champagne and broken china and glass.

After seeing James blow away the machine gunner at the door, a pair of thugs had overturned the banquet table to use it as a shield. James glimpsed the thick metal tube of a shotgun barrel with a grooved wooden grip protruding from the side. He could only guess what the other hood might be armed with. The shotgun was enough to convince him to stay behind the cover of the doorway.

The shotgun boomed, buckshot smashing into the French doors, shattering glass and whining against the framework. James shielded his face with a forearm and a moment later, a flying shard of glass snagged the sleeve of his dinner jacket.

Katz jogged to the doors, carrying the Sterling subgun discarded by a slain opponent. The Israeli braced the weapon across his prosthetic right arm with the pistol-grip in his left fist. Manning followed, Magnum revolvers in his fists. Having seen and heard the shotgun blast, they approached the doors cautiously.

"Two guys behind a table," James told them. "Roughly two o'clock. Not sure what kinda firepower they've—"

Another blast tore into the doorway. More glass burst across the threshold, and shotgun pellets screeched through the opening. Katz dropped to one knee and fired the Sterling where James had directed, spraying the upper right corner of the room with 9 mm rounds. The Phoenix commander glimpsed the table and the shotgunner—who fell backward, blood and brains dripping from his skull. At least one parabellum slug had torn through the guy's upper face.

Manning stood over Katz and, feeling a bit like a character in an old cowboy movie, fired the revolvers, right hand and left hand, and repeated the salvo. Four .357 rounds splintered the tabletop. Bits of wood went flying, and the echo of the booming handguns all but drowned out the scream of the man hidden behind the table.

The three Phoenix warriors entered the ballroom; Katz rushed in first, while Manning and James covered his advance. The Canadian fighter entered next.

James jammed the Largo pistol into his belt and scooped up the fallen FMK-3 submachine gun as he followed his partners.

There were no living opponents in the ballroom, but the roar of automatic fire continued in the hallway. A bloodied figure, clad in a red jacket, hurtled from the hall to the ballroom. There were three bullet holes in his chest and bloodstains on his white shirt. An unfired pistol slipped from the dead man's fingers.

"Hello, mates," David McCarter announced as he appeared in the hall. The Briton pointed the muzzle of his Ingram machine pistol at the ceiling. Smoke curled from the end of the barrel. "I see you chaps have been busy."

"It hasn't been dull," Katz replied, canting the Sterling subgun across his left shoulder. "How are things going out front?"

"Lots of cars were speeding out of this place by the time we arrived," McCarter answered. "We stopped a couple of 'em, and the cops formed a roadblock to stop a few others. At least two cars got away. Probably more."

"I hope you got Cercueil and Penn," James commented as he approached the banquet table. The two blood-spattered corpses wouldn't improve anyone's appetite.

"Where's Rafael?" Manning asked, gathering up the dead shotgunner's weapon. It was a Winchester riot gun, a 12-gauge pump with an extended 6-round tubular magazine.

"He's helping the cops and the CIS lads check the rest of the house," McCarter explained. "Doesn't sound like they found more hired guns lurkin' about. Guess we're finished here."

"Not quite," Katz declared. "We've still got to search this house for evidence even if we were lucky enough to catch Cercueil and Penn before they could flee the area."

"Might have caught Penn," James said with a sigh. "But I bet Cercueil was in the first fuckin' car to light outta here."

"We'll find out soon enough," Katz stated, taking advantage of the chance to light up a Camel cigarette. "We've got another problem to look into. One of Penn's men mentioned something odd about the sugarcane fields."

"You think there's something out there?" McCarter asked.

"The man was afraid to go into the field," Katz explained. "He said, 'Those things are out there.' Maybe we'd better find out what he meant."

"Maybe we'd be happier if we didn't know," Manning said grimly, bracing the shotgun across his shoulder.

## 11

The tall stalks of sugarcane swayed slightly as a cool breeze swept over them. A chilly wind in Jamaica was unusual at that time of year. The five men of Phoenix Force wondered if the breeze was really cold or if the chill came from within.

The field seemed to have a sinister atmosphere, as though a malevolent presence was brooding among the sugarcane stalks. The commandos could see little beyond the acres of towering crops. Anything could be hidden among the forest of sugarcane, which stood five to ten feet high. A Sherman tank could have been concealed in that field.

"What the hell are we looking for?" Sergeant Bristol demanded as he followed the Phoenix team through the dense crop of rigid stalks.

"Something that might be able to hear us," Calvin James hissed, gripping the confiscated FMK-3 subgun in his fists. "Maybe something that'll try to kill us."

"The prisoners said there's nothing out here but a couple empty buildings," another Kingston cop named Garner commented. The young patrolman held a riot gun similar to the weapon Manning had taken from a dead hoodlum in the house. "A storage house for tools and machinery to work the fields and a sort of barracks for the hired laborers during the cutting season.''

"Either shut up or go back," David McCarter said in a tense whisper. Ingram held ready, the Briton turned suddenly when some sugarcane rustled.

A large brown rat scurried between two stalks. McCarter held his fire. His heartbeat was rapid, and he felt the blood rushing through his brain. Excitement and expectation had mingled with a trace of terror. It was a familiar sensation for McCarter; a thrilling sensation that he needed in his life on a regular basis.

Gary Manning was leading the group: the Canadian demolitions expert was an expert at detecting booby traps, especially devices rigged to explosives. Encizo and Manning followed close behind, scanning the area for trip wires and pressure plates. They looked for sugarcane stalks that might have been rigged to trigger a concealed trapgun, or for patches of overturned earth that might have covered a pit filled with sharpened stakes.

The five Phoenix warriors were constantly alert to possible danger, more so than Bristol and the three other Kingston police officers who accompanied them who were unfamiliar with this sort of situation. The sugarcane fields were almost a miniature jungle, a different world than the concrete-and-glass cities the cops were accustomed to. Katz glanced over his shoulder at the cops and shook his head. He wished he had not agreed to let them trek through the cane fields with Phoenix Force. The four policemen were more apt to be a liability than an asset.

Manning peered through the two-inch-thick stalks that towered above the moist ground. Seeing a long one-story wooden building with a tar-paper roof ahead, he gestured to the others. The structure appeared to be the workers' quarters. Katz nodded at Manning and likewise signaled to Encizo and McCarter, tilting his head to indicate the building.

The three chosen warriors crept forward while Katz, James and the four cops covered them from the shelter of the sugarcane. Manning, Encizo and McCarter spread out as they stepped into the clearing and approached the barracks. Better able to view the building without the multijointed cane stalks blocking their view, the trio discovered the windows were blacked out by thick boards nailed on the outside of the billets. The front door was bolted by a heavy beam and secured by two thick steel padlocks.

"Bloody hell," McCarter rasped softly. The trace of terror was growing fast and threatened to outweigh the excitement and anticipation he felt. "What have they got in there?"

"I'll take care of the locks," Encizo whispered, removing a small leather packet from his pocket. "Somebody check the rear."

"I'll cover it," Manning volunteered.

The Canadian moved around the building to the back, finding blank walls and more boarded-up windows. There was no back door, but he stayed in position anyway. He moved to one of the shuttered windows and listened for the telltale sound of voices, machinery or footsteps. His eyes widened when he heard a strange gurgling, like that of an infant trying to speak. A low, mournful groan made Manning's stomach knot in a cold, hard ball. He clutched the steel frame of the riot gun and held his breath as he waited for Encizo to pick the locks to the door.

Encizo easily unlocked the padlocks with a thin metal pick and a narrow hacksaw blade. He worked the probes inside the keyhole of the first lock for less than ten seconds, and the shackle popped open. The second padlock required less than half that time.

Removing the padlocks from the hasps, Encizo stopped and reached for the MP-5 machine pistol that hung from a shoulder strap. An odd scraping sound at the opposite side of the door had surprised the Cuban. He glanced up at McCarter and noticed the British ace was gripping his Ingram M-10 a bit tighter than usual. McCarter had heard it, too.

*I wonder if Pandora felt this way when she opened the box that unleashed evil upon the earth,* Encizo thought grimly as he removed the last padlock and prepared to raise the beam from the door. Low moans from within the building almost convinced him to leave the door bolted. Yet the sound relayed suffering, and Encizo had known too much suffering not to feel compassion toward others in this condition. Nonetheless, the groans seemed threatening, as if he was about to open a cage filled with dangerous wounded beasts.

Encizo swallowed his fear and removed the bolt.

The door burst open, nearly striking Encizo. McCarter aimed his M-10 at the doorway as a scrawny shape clad in filthy rags staggered across the threshold. Eyes like glass marbles stared from the emaciated dark features of the repulsive figure shuffling barefoot from the building. Spittle dripped from the quivering lips as its unblinking gaze turned toward McCarter.

"Oh, my God," the Briton whispered, ice scorpions crawling up his spine as he stared directly into the face of the zombie.

A flicker of consciousness appeared in the creature's glassy eyes. The zombie growled like a beast and raised its right arm. The long, curved blade of a sickle extended from its fist.

McCarter triggered his Ingram. A 3-round burst tore through the zombie's chest. Its body jerked from the impact, blood oozing from the ragged holes in its tattered shirt. The creature staggered backward but did not fall. More moaning horrors shuffled from the barracks. Encizo tried to slam the door, but too many of the zombies were pressed against it for him to hold them at bay.

The thing McCarter had shot staggered toward him once more, crimson drool spilling from its open mouth. The Briton clenched his teeth, raised his Ingram and fired. Parabellums pulped the zombie's face and exploded the back of its skull. Lifeless, the creature collapsed, but other nightmare figures continued to march woodenly from the workers' quarters.

"Lord Jesus Christ," Sergeant Bristol gasped as he stared at the bizarre scene from the cover of the sugarcane stalks. He could have been uttering a blasphemous oath or a prayer for salvation. Perhaps a combination of both.

Calvin James could not fault Bristol either way. The tough guy from Chicago watched the dreadful, mindless creatures shuffle from the building. The scene was right out of a horror movie. More than a dozen blank-eyed human scarecrows emerged from the building. They were men and yet not men, human and yet not human. Their minds and willpower had been destroyed and replaced by whatever instructions Cercueil and his followers had programmed into them.

Whatever else they might be—human, subhuman or flesh-and-blood robots—the zombies were dangerous. Armed with machetes, sickles and hoes, they seemed ready to lash out at anyone who appeared to be unlike their kind. Several zombies raised their weapons and charged McCarter and Encizo.

Backing away from the advancing figures, the British and Cuban warriors opened fire. Parabellum slugs ripped into the torsos of three approaching zombies. Bleeding bodies staggered backward into other brain-damaged androids. Only one creature suffered enough internal damage to heart and lungs to collapse. The others moved forward, including two opponents with blood trickling from bullet holes in their chests.

"The bastards are immune to pain!" McCarter exclaimed. "Go for the heads!"

The booming report of a shotgun announced that Gary Manning had joined the battle. The Canadian had hurriedly returned from behind the building when he'd heard the first gunshots and had practically run straight into a group of zombies. Manning saw one figure raise a machete and opened fire. The force of the powerful 12-gauge weapon blasted the emaciated creature off its feet and pitched it back five feet. It crashed to the earth, upper torso ripped into shreds.

McCarter and Encizo fired their machine pistols again. Zombie skulls burst apart from multiple 9 mm bullets. The slain zombies fell, but the others, apparently unconcerned with the fate of their comrades and devoid of any fear of injury or death, continued to advance.

"Bristol!" Katz called out to the Jamaican police sergeant. "You and your men wait here and back us up. Hold your fire until—"

The Phoenix commander's warning came too late to stop Officer Garner from opening fire with his riot gun. The cop's eyes swelled with horror as he stared at the zombies; he mumbled something in a hysterical manner, words tumbling together too rapidly to make sense. Although every man in the unit had realized they might find these terrible yet pathetic creatures lurking in the cane fields, the idea of encountering zombies had seemed too bizarre to be real. The horror of actually finding a group of beings straight out of voodoo folklore had stunned every member of the team. Even the ultraprofessional Katzenelenbogen, despite his decades of training and experience, hadn't been prepared for the sight.

It was too much for Garner. The panic-stricken cop responded to his terror by firing his 12-gauge relentlessly at the zombies. Buckshot burst from the short-barreled shotgun. Pellets tore into the shoulder and face of one zombie and into the upper back of another. Both ragged figures spun around from the blast. Only one went down, its spinal cord severed. The other creature remained upright, although blood appeared on the tattered sleeve of its filthy cotton shirt. The right side of its face had been pulverized by buckshot, the eyeball dangling on its bloodied cheek by the stem of the optic nerve.

"Stop it!" James shouted as he rushed toward Garner.

He was not concerned about the welfare of the zombies. James was afraid Garner might hit McCarter or Encizo with an indiscriminate burst of shotgun pellets. The cop pumped his weapon again and fired another blast at the sinister horde. James closed in and karated Garner's forearm to numb the ulnar nerve and prevent the cop from working the trigger of his shotgun.

James also swatted the back of his hand across the policeman's face. It was a crude method of jolting the hysterics from the terrified Garner, but there was no time for subtle tactics. However, James had not been able to stop Garner from firing a second blast.

A few pellets tore chunks of flesh from the arm of one zombie and slammed into the rib cage of another. Garner's buckshot also hammered the box-shaped frame of the Ingram M-10 machine pistol in McCarter's fists. The impact kicked the gun out of the Briton's hands.

"Damn!" McCarter rasped, his hands quivering from the unexpected force that had plucked his weapon from his grasp.

Luckily, none of the pellets had claimed a finger in the process. That was about all the British ace had any reason to feel thankful for. Two slobbering zombies were headed toward him. The taller of the pair wielded a machete, while the other creature held a hoe with a rusty front blade. Their dark, corpselike features revealed little expression except a wild animal fury displayed in the open, gaping eyes.

Encizo was busy hosing down another pair of zombie opponents with his MP-5. He saw the pair crumple and swung his Heckler & Koch toward the two monstrous figures that threatened McCarter.

A quick salvo from his gun penetrated the skull of the closest zombie, smashing through the thing's head with ease. The zombie half turned and fell, landing on what remained of its face. The body barely twitched as death claimed another subject. The zombies were half dead and looked to be completely beyond redemption and "rehabilitation." Whatever humanity they possessed probably welcomed an end to their miserable half life.

As Encizo trained his MP-5 on the tall, machete-wielding figure that was about to attack McCarter, its sinister brethren swung a hoe at the Cuban warrior.

The attack was clumsy. The drugs and physical abuse used to destroy the willpower of the zombies had also ruined their coordination. The blade of the hoe missed Encizo's head but snared the frame of his machine pistol.

The violent tug deflected Encizo's weapon away from its intended target. Now, ironically, the MP-5 was pointed at the chest of the zombie with the hoe. With a pull of the trigger, Encizo sent a volley of 9 mm rounds into the creature. The zombie fell backward, and the hoe, which was still hooked over Encizo's H&K blaster, caused the machine pistol to slip from the warrior's hands.

*"¡Cristo!"* the Cuban exclaimed as a sickle-swinging zombie executed a backhand sweep, the long, curved blade aimed at Encizo's neck.

The Phoenix pro ducked under the whirling crescent of sharp steel. The sickle sliced through air above Encizo's bowed head. He chose not to think about how close the blade had come to removing the top of his skull. The full terror of this close brush with death would not sink in until later, when he was not completely absorbed with survival. At the moment there was no time to reflect on the situation. There was only time to react to the threat.

Encizo instinctively grabbed the hilt of the Cold Steel Tanto knife on his belt instead of reaching for the H&K P9S autoloader holstered under his left arm. The Cuban had been a knife fighter since childhood and still favored the blade for extremely close combat. He also knew he could draw the Tanto from its sheath, naked blade ready for battle, faster than he could draw the pistol, snap off the safety catch and point and squeeze the trigger.

The zombie raised its sickle for another attack. Encizo lunged. The slanted tip of the Cold Steel blade slid easily into his opponent's solar plexus. His free hand grappled to release the sickle from the zombie's grip. Again he shoved the knife into the creature's flesh. It drove upward into the chest cavity. The technique, which Encizo had used many times previously, had never failed to bring down an enemy.

Until now.

The zombie did not respond to the knife thrust. Despite massive internal damage, it did not feel pain or shock. The creature did not appear to realize it was dying—or perhaps it did not care. But it still intended to take out Rafael Encizo.

The Cuban felt the beast struggle to overcome the handicap of four inches of sharp steel buried in its chest. The emaciated man-thing was stronger than it looked, but malnutrition and years of physical abuse had taken its toll. It had formerly been a skid-row wino whom Cercueil's people had abducted and transformed into the present mindless being that struggled against Encizo. It had strength limited to the extent of its aroused fury, and not much endurance.

Encizo restrained the zombie's sickle with one hand and worked the handle of the Tanto with the other. He jerked the hilt up, down and sideways, both to increase the damage to his opponent's body tissues and to wiggle the blade free. The zombie's free hand reached for Encizo's face. Dirty fingers pawed at the Cuban's mouth and nose. Broken black nails crept toward his eyes.

The Phoenix fighter turned his face away, released the knife handle, and batted the groping hand aside with a forearm blow. He glimpsed the zombie's face. The eyes were filled with demented rage, and blood issued from the creature's nostrils and mouth, from which a series of monotonous animal grunts poured forth. Encizo slammed his fist into those terrible features. The monstrous head bounced from the punch, and the equally monstrous body swayed.

Encizo grabbed the knife handle once more and yanked with strength born of desperation. The blade came free with a sickening slushing sound of wet flesh and gurgling blood. Crimson splashed Encizo's shirt-front, but he barely noticed as he shoved the zombie with two hands. The creature staggered backward, still staring at Encizo, its knees finally buckling as the loss of blood robbed it of its remaining strength. Then the man-thing wilted to the ground.

Threatened by a tall zombie with a machete, David McCarter had been too busy to come to his partner's assistance. The android swung its jungle knife at the agile ex-SAS commando, who dodged it and grabbed the half-human wrist before the creature could try another stroke.

Twisting the wrist, McCarter swung a boot under the zombie's extended arm, kicking the creature in the lower abdomen. The animal did not even grunt in response. McCarter could not worry about his choice of tactics. He played out his move and prayed it would work.

The Briton held the zombie's wrist with one hand and grabbed the upper forearm with the other. He shoved down with two hands and smashed the zombie's forearm across a bent knee. The radius bone snapped and poked sharply through the skin of the creature's forearm. The zombie did not appear to feel any pain, but the fingers opened, the machete fell at McCarter's feet, and the broken limb swung limply aside.

Then the Phoenix crusader executed a high kick to the zombie's face. The creature's head snapped back with such force that two neck vertebrae popped. The shock to the spinal cord and brain stem was too much for even a zombie to endure, and he dropped like a steer in a slaughterhouse.

Another zombie, armed with a rusty sickle, shuffled toward McCarter as the Briton scooped up the machete. The creature swung. The sickle arched widely over McCarter's head. The Briton grabbed the machete and, utilizing the momentum established by the creature, turned the weapon so that the sharp edge chopped into the zombie's skull. The blade split bone and destroyed the creature's brain.

"Now be off!" McCarter snarled with a kind of fearful disgust at what is grossly unnatural and kicked the zombie away.

He landed the boot to its chest as if kicking in a door. The blow sent the corpse hurtling backward into yet more zombies. McCarter pulled his Browning Hi-

Power from shoulder leather. The familiar feel of the 9 mm pistol in his grasp sent a hot flush of renewed confidence through him.

Gary Manning's shotgun boomed, and the corpse of a ragged zombie crash-landed among its mindless peers. The Canadian hastily worked the pump action, eliminating two more opponents. Manning felt trapped in the middle of a nightmare as zombie fingers closed around the barrel of his Winchester riot gun. A hideous face stared at him. The eyes were like those of the killer wolves he had encountered in Finland, half crazy with desperation and starvation.

Manning thrust the muzzle of the shotgun under the zombie's chin and squeezed the trigger. Buckshot exploded from the barrel, and the zombie's head burst into a spectacular nova of blood. Just then, as if on cue, another opponent swung a machete at the Canadian's head.

Combat-honed reflexes saved Gary Manning. Metal rang against metal as he whipped the barrel of the shotgun into the advancing blade and blocked the machete stroke. He quickly executed a butt-stroke with the walnut stock of the riot gun. Wood crashed into the side of the zombie's skull. A hairline fracture rendered the "walking dead man" unconscious. The zombie dropped silently to the ground.

Manning was about to load another shell into the breech of his shotgun. A zombie interrupted him by rudely swinging a sickle in a wild overhead stroke. Manning raised the riot gun, holding the barrel in one fist and the stock in the other. The steel frame formed a solid bar that blocked the sickle blade.

The zombie's demented facial features reflected an expression similar to surprise. The Canadian pushed the frame of his weapon against the sickle blade to shove the weapon-tool away. Stepping forward and dropping to one knee, Manning slashed the barrel of the Winchester at the zombie's bony ankles, sweeping the creature off its feet. Manning jumped up. He quickly stamped the butt of the shotgun into the forehead of the horrid opponent, caving in the frontal bone of the humanoid's skull.

Katz and James had also joined the battle, rushing from the sugarcane to assist their companions. The two had seen enough to realize threatening the zombies or shooting over their heads would be as useless as attempting such tactics against a volcano spewing hot lava. Neither would torso shots effectively stop the zombies. The only sure way of dealing with these creatures was to attack the brain.

Rifles with night scopes might have allowed them to deal with the zombies from a distance, but Katz and James were armed with relatively unfamiliar submachine guns designed for close-quarter rapid-fire fighting rather than for distance and accuracy. They had to get closer. Much closer.

Two zombies turned toward James and Katz as they darted into the open. One of the creatures had been the victim of Garner's panicky shotgun blast; half its face was ripped open, with an eyeball hanging from a torn socket. James raised his FMK-3 subgun and destroyed what remained of the mutilated face. The corpse slumped to the ground. Katz fired his Sterling a microsecond later, and the second zombie fell across the first.

Four humanoids staggered toward Garner in the sugarcane, attracted by the booming report of his shotgun. The terrified cop was once again peppering the creatures with pellets before they were within killing range. Torn and bloodied, the zombies would eventually collapse from the shotgun blasts, but the damage was not forceful or abrupt enough to bring them down.

Sergeant Bristol yelled at Garner to hold his fire. The patrolman didn't pay attention. He was trapped in the nightmare that had marched from the laborers' quarters. Bristol glanced around and discovered that one of the three policemen in his charge had apparently bolted in terror and abandoned the team, retreating deeper into the cane fields.

The remaining man under Bristol's command waited tensely for the walking terror to close in. Officer Thompson's face dripped with sweat, and his eyes seemed ready to burst from their sockets, but he hadn't panicked. Bristol certainly didn't blame the man for being afraid. Thompson looked about as frightened as Bristol felt. The sergeant was glad he could not see his own face at that moment, for he was certain it would also be a mask of utter fear.

"Now!" Bristol shouted, and fired his riot gun point-blank at the face of the closest zombie.

The creature's head mushroomed in a spray of red and gray. Thompson fired his shotgun a split second later, and another decapitated zombie collapsed. Only one human robot eventually fell from all the buckshot fired by the frenzied Garner. The last of the four figures, a machete clenched in its fists, lumbered directly for Garner.

Garner worked the pump of his riot gun, aimed and pulled the trigger. A dull click was the only response. He had burned up all his shells. Screaming he spun around to escape—and ran headlong into a pair of eight-foot-high cane stalks.

Dazed and terrified, he staggered away and turned to see the zombie raise its machete. Garner screamed once more before the sharp steel blade split his face open, then he fell lifelessly. The zombie repeatedly swung the jungle knife, chopping the unresisting flesh.

"My God!" Bristol exclaimed, charging to the spot.

The zombie continued to hack away at the bloodied lump that formerly had been Officer Garner, and didn't notice Bristol. It didn't turn when the sergeant raised his riot gun. A burst of buckshot dispatched the creature, ending the horrible sight.

Bristol backed away, his stomach convulsing with pure repulsion. He heard an ugly choking sound and liquid poured onto the ground. Officer Thompson was vomiting. Bristol resisted the urge to follow his example and turned to see how Phoenix Force was faring.

Katz and James helped their partners finish off the last of the voodoo horror-story creatures. The clearing was covered with a grisly carpet of mangled, gory flesh. Yet the five commandos seemed to pay little attention to the grotesque debris. McCarter yanked the pin from his SAS flash-bang grenade and tossed it into the building. They stood clear of the doorway until the concussion blast exploded. Then McCarter and Manning rushed inside while the others covered them from the doorway. The British and Canadian warriors emerged less than a minute later, weapons canted on their shoulders.

"Empty," McCarter announced as he leaned against the doorway and removed a pack of Player's from his pocket. His fingers shook slightly as he withdrew a cigarette, but his hands were steady by the time he held the flame of his lighter to the tip of the Player's. "Guess we got them all."

"Don't bet on it," Calvin James replied grimly. "This mission ain't over yet."

## 12

"Zombies?" Colonel Wells glared disbelievingly at Katz, James and Bristol as if he thought they had all gone mad. "Carlos de Madrid had an army of zombies at his plantation?"

"If I hadn't seen it myself," Bristol said, "I don't think I'd believe it, either, sir."

"We knew about the graveyard ghoulie the cops shot at the hotel a couple of days ago," James remarked, sprawled in a chair in Lieutenant Smith's office. "Not really surprising to discover there were more of them around. Sure as hell was scary to come up against more than twenty of those things in the cane fields."

"What were they doing there?" Wells demanded, spreading his hands in an exaggerated gesture of helplessness. "De Madrid was a sugarcane plantation owner, not a voodoo witch doctor."

"Well, Cercueil had to hide his zombies somewhere until he needed them for hit jobs," Yakov Katzenelenbogen began, sipping lukewarm tea from a cup. "The plantation was really an ideal location. Few witnesses, and most of those would be Penn's hired thugs. How many other people would be curious about laborers in the cane fields? Who would suspect the scrawny poor devils chopping down sugarcane were zombies?''

"Cercueil had a safe house for his zombies, and de Madrid got free slave labor," James muttered in disgust. "Those two bastards probably figured it was a perfect arrangement."

"There have been stories about this sort of thing for almost a hundred years in Haiti," Della Walkins added as she sat in a chair next to James. "Tales of wealthy plantation owners and farmers using zombies to work their fields. Of course, these stories were generally regarded as myths because the idea of walking dead men turned into slaves by voodoo magic is simply too absurd to consider."

"Maybe some of those stories were true," James declared. "Herbal medicine, knowing how to grind up roots, minerals, plant stems, leaves, animal matter and stuff like that for ointments and potions has always been a part of so-called occult skills. Alchemists, early physicians and witch doctors all studied herbs and chemicals. Voodoo *bocors* may have learned how to make drugs to destroy willpower. A lot of poisons and narcotics are found in plants. Zombies may have been around for decades, but nobody has taken them seriously because legends claimed they were reanimated corpses."

"Fascinating theory," Colonel Wells said without much enthusiasm. "But I'm more concerned about our present problems. The police caught a number of de Madrid's party guests, but they didn't get Montgomery Penn or this Haitian gangster. Cercueil?''

"He's not a gangster," Katz warned. "He doesn't think like a hoodlum. Cercueil was probably a high-ranking officer in the Ton Ton Macoute. Men who belong to secret police organizations always consider themselves to be patriots and justify their vicious behavior as necessary for national security."

"Whatever he is or *thinks* himself to be," Wells said in exasperation, "the Haitian got away last night. You had him and he slipped through your fingers, Mr. Gray. All you and your group have accomplished since you arrived has been to increase the number of dead bodies in Jamaica."

"Gee," James snorted. "I didn't really notice anybody cryin' their eyes out because a bunch of low-life gangsters and two-bit buttonmen got wasted."

"Do you forget that a police officer was killed?" Wells demanded. "He was hacked to pieces by one of those supposed zombies."

"We all knew the raid would be dangerous, Colonel," Bristol declared. "Officer Garner knew it, too."

"I'm surprised that you're defending these people, Sergeant," Wells remarked. "Garner was one of your men. According to your report on his death, Garner was a bloody hero."

"True," Bristol said with a nod. "He was killed when he came to rescue me. Garner should be buried with full honors, and his family should know how very proud we were to have him on the force."

Calvin James pretended to scratch his mustache to conceal a smile. He did not find Bristol's remark amusing, although the sergeant was less than accurate about Garner's "heroism." James smiled with a sense of warm satisfaction because he understood why Bristol had lied about Garner. The Kingston cop had displayed a part of his personality none of Phoenix Force had seen before. A part that compelled Bristol to sacrifice a bit of personal glory in order to protect the reputation of one of his men. Sergeant Bristol might just be a good guy, after all.

"I don't think Garner would want us to quit now, Colonel," Bristol continued. "Let's not allow his sacrifice to be in vain."

"Sorry, Sergeant." Wells shook his head. "I still feel I must contact the governor-general and advise him to tell the President of the United States to recall Mr. Gray and his team. The body count since they arrived is extraordinary. Almost forty people were killed at de Madrid's estate last night . . . including the men you all claim were zombies. Let me remind you, gentlemen: whatever you choose to call them, they were still human beings."

"They really didn't leave us much choice of action," Katz remarked, finishing his tea and lighting up a Camel cigarette. "If we leave, Colonel, what do you intend to do? Pretend Cercueil doesn't exist? Hope he decides to give up his plans and quits killing American tourists and innocent Jamaicans?"

"He has a point, sir," Bristol added. "We can criticize some of their tactics, but Mr. Gray and his group have been more successful than either the police or your office, Colonel. We didn't learn about Cercueil or Penn. They did.''

"So you think they should stay?'' Wells inquired.

"I don't really like admitting they've handled this better than my own police department,'' Bristol said with a sigh. "Yet what matters is solving this mess once and for all.''

"What do you think, Sergeant Walkins?'' Wells asked the lady cop.

"I agree with Sergeant Bristol,'' Della answered, glancing at James. "I think we can accomplish a lot more with their assistance than without it.''

"Very well,'' the colonel said, frowning. "I'll advise the governor-general to grant you fellows another forty-eight hours. You'd damn well better have some positive results by then or I'll see to it you're out of Jamaica on the next plane if I have to escort you to the airport at gunpoint.''

Bristol nearly scoffed at that remark. Wells had never seen the mysterious five commandos in action. They handled weapons as if they had been born with guns and knives in their fists. Wells attempting to threaten them with a firearm would probably frighten the five fighting machines about as much as a barking poodle would intimidate a Bengal tiger.

"Forty-eight hours.'' Katz nodded in agreement. "With a bit of luck, we can wrap this up in two days. Providing we can locate Cercueil again.''

"Any idea where to start looking?'' Bristol inquired.

"Our partners are working on that right now," the Israeli answered, gingerly scratching his right cheek with a curved point of the three-hook prosthesis. "They're checking on several possible leads."

"Such as?" Wells asked, cocking an eyebrow.

"Questioning the guests from de Madrid's party," Calvin James explained. "Pretty standard cop stuff. It's sort of a long shot, but there's a possibility some of de Madrid's friends might know some details about Cercueil or Penn."

"We suspect we'll be more apt to find more information about Penn than Cercueil," Katz added. "He's been here much longer than the Haitians. It's logical people would know more about Penn's activities. Several of de Madrid's visitors appeared to be accustomed to cocaine and expensive ladies of the evening. Both were probably supplied by Penn. Perhaps one or more of these individuals will be willing to give us information about the gangster to avoid the embarrassment and the unpleasant publicity of a trial for their involvement at de Madrid's party."

"Not to mention avoiding prison if enough charges can be made to send 'em to the big house," James commented. "Might be kinda hard to convince some of those dudes that they won't be able to weasel outta this. They've got money and influence. Folks like that are used to doing pretty much what they please."

"Carlos de Madrid was a wealthy man with a lot of influence, too," Wells said grimly. "My office is going to get a lot of flak when news of his death becomes public. He had friends in the export trade and in government. There's bound to be some heat when they learn he was killed during a raid on his home."

"I don't think you need to worry about that," Katz stated. "Not when all the details are known. I doubt anyone will want to admit they were friends with a man who was involved in everything from black-markcteering and narcotics to conspiracy to commit murder and possibly even an attempt to overthrow the Jamaican government."

"What?" Wells glared at Katz as if he thought the Israeli might be making some sort of sick joke.

"That may very well be part of Cercueil's plan," Katz explained. "Murdering American tourists was just part of the conspiracy. We've encountered ex-Ton Ton Macoute terrorist leaders before. They don't go to this sort of trouble to kill people just for entertainment. They have something much bigger in mind."

"But a government takeover?" Wells shook his head.

"Look," Katz began, "Jamaica needs a strong tourist trade for a sound economy. If Cercueil can ruin American tourism to Jamaica it will virtually destroy the trade. If he can ruin relations between the United States and Jamaica, your country will be in even worse shape. Next, you'll have increased internal violence with leftists blaming right-wingers and vice versa."

"Meantime, Cercueil is building a secret empire made up of criminals and obeah cults," James added. "While everyone else is fighting among themselves, Cercueil waits for an opportunity to move in and take over."

"That's a pretty farfetched theory," Wells said with a frown.

"Not when you consider the fact we're dealing with the Ton Ton Macoute," Katz declared. "Cercueil is a veteran of a totalitarian system that worked successfully for almost thirty years in Haiti. One reason it worked was because the criminal elements in Haiti were often connected with the government. That's not really so incredible. Governments make deals with gangsters all the time. Police in every country operate in this manner. Don't forget, the Ton Ton Macoute was a type of national police force in Haiti."

"Cercueil is also trying to gain support among the obeah voodoo cults," James added. "That's another page from Papa Doc's book on how to be supreme dictator. Old Francois Duvalier was far better at using the voodoo tricks than his son. Maybe that's why Baby Doc didn't stay in power nearly as long as his daddy."

"Cal's right," Della said with a nod, giving James a brief smile. "The ruling powers in Haiti always took advantage of the population's belief in voodoo."

"I thought most Haitians had been converted to Catholicism," Wells remarked. "Voodoo is supposed to be a thing of the past."

"Voodoo is a hybrid religion," Della explained. "It's a combination of animist beliefs from Africa and Christianity, with a lot of European witchcraft practices thrown in. A Haitian might call himself a Catholic, yet still believe in voodoo. Catholic saints may also represent voodooistic gods to a Haitian. Most people are apt to dismiss voodoo as just a superstitious cult, but it is really a religion with more in common with Christianity than one might think."

"But Duvalier manipulated his people," Wells insisted. "He preyed on their superstitions and fears." He seemed uneasy at this comparison of Christianity and voodooism.

"Just as the Catholic church did in Spain during the Inquisition," Della said with a shrug. "Or as the ayatollah does with his Shiite Moslem followers in Iran. Aren't there a number of American evangelists on television, mostly Protestants, who are always warning about the last days and the coming of the Antichrist?"

"They talk about other stuff, too," James answered. "Mostly how they need more money to keep their shows on the air."

"You're not seriously comparing Duvalier to a TV evangelist, Sergeant Walkins?" Wells demanded.

"Of course not," she answered. "The goals and motives are entirely different, but the method of manipulating people by appealing to the fears built into their belief system is similar."

"I think the sergeant has a good point," Katz stated. "Cercueil's methods are not unlike those of Duvalier or hundreds of other political or religious leaders who have succeeded in conquests in the past. Farfetched or not, Cercueil's plan could succeed if events unfold in his favor. Even if he fails, a lot of innocent people will suffer if he isn't stopped."

"He's already got a lot of innocent blood on his hands," James said. "Son of a bitch isn't gonna get away with that."

"We'll have to find him first," Bristol commented. "De Madrid's party guests may not be much help. Aren't your people working on other sources, Gray?"

"Sanchez is trying to contact Kevinson," Katz answered. "The black marketeer seems to have gone into hiding. No doubt he's afraid Penn will be after him, having vouched for the three 'bankers' from Martinique. I just hope we find him before Penn does."

"Do you think he'll cooperate with us?" Wells asked.

"Does he have a choice?" James replied with a shrug. "Kevinson can play ball with us and stay alive and outta prison or he can take his chances alone against Penn. That ain't much of a choice."

"According to the Kingston police records, Penn has a mistress . . . or at least she used to be his regular girlfriend," James said. "A former airline stewardess from Sweden. Can't remember her name. Sounded phony anyway."

"Inger Blomgren," Katz supplied, tapping into his near-photographic memory. "Apparently she got mixed up with Penn a couple years ago, quit the airline and set up house here. The police have no evidence linking her to any criminal activity except her close association with Penn. There's a possibility she might know some of the places where Penn might go to keep a low profile when the authorities are looking for him.''

"Penn wouldn't be stupid enough to share any real secrets about his business with this Swedish whore,'' Bristol declared, shaking his head. "Your people are grasping for straws, Gray.''

"Perhaps,'' the Phoenix Force commander said. "But you'd be surprised how many men reveal secrets to girlfriends, mistresses and other lovers. Men will sometimes get quite careless with a woman, especially after a few drinks. That's why the Soviet KGB trains female agents called 'swallows' who seduce men to get information.''

"Hopefully, one of your ideas will work,'' Wells said, with much doubt evident in his tone. "This entire affair has become bloodier and potentially far more volatile than anyone could have realized. So far, we don't have much reason to be pleased with your results, Mr. Gray. You'd better succeed in your mission, and quickly.''

"I agree,'' Katz said, expressing little concern about Wells's thinly veiled threat. "Not for the reasons that seem to worry you, but because Cercueil isn't going to sit around waiting for us to find him. If we don't locate him soon, he'll escape and we might never get him then. At least not until it's too late.''

"Too late for whom?'' Wells inquired.

"For all of us,'' the Israeli replied. "If, God forbid, he should succeed, the ultimate results could only be catastrophic, not only for Haiti and her neighbors, but for every country in the Western hemisphere.''

## 13

Kingston, Jamaica, is a modern city with towering skyscrapers and office buildings, flashy discos and glitzy night clubs. After driving through the city, Gary Manning and Lieutenant Smith arrived at a great square structure of concrete and glass known as the Brentwood Apartments. The high rise was located among an assortment of shops, restaurants and traditional English pubs.

"This place looks expensive," Manning remarked as he gazed up at the building.

"Quite," Smith agreed stiffly. The stuffed shirt cop did not seem to care for his current task of chauffeuring Manning around the city. "Penn can afford to give his sluts the very best. You notice the shrubbery on the roof?"

"Yeah, I can see a bit of it, along the edge. Looks like dwarf trees and rosebushes," the Canadian commando answered, shielding his eyes with the palm of a hand. The midday sun burned brightly above the apartment house. "Rooftop garden?"

"Probably a restaurant as well," Smith stated as they walked to the entrance. "Rooftop restaurants are popular in Kingston. They are something of a status symbol for hotels and sky-rises here. Many of the more expensive places feature such restaurants.''

"Maybe we'll get lucky and find Inger Blomgren having lunch with Montgomery Penn up there,'' Manning remarked, although he did not sound very hopeful that would happen.

They found the manager's office in the lobby. Smith flashed his badge, told the manager he was there on official business, and confided he needed to speak to Inger Blomgren. The manager immediately gave him the apartment number and a passkey. Manning noticed the manager seemed very nervous but not very surprised by their visit. He guessed the manager had always suspected Ms. Blomgren was associated with unsavory characters and that the guy was probably afraid he might catch some of the hell when they lowered the boom on his tenant.

Smith headed for the elevator, but Manning insisted they use the stairs instead. The Kingston cop was annoyed by this and considered Manning downright paranoid. The Canadian demolitions expert did not give a damn what Smith thought. He knew how easily an elevator could be booby-trapped or sabotaged at a moment's notice. If the manager or someone else in the lobby was working for the enemy, a phone call could warn the Blomgren woman and whoever might be with her.

If that happened, the woman might try to flee or contact Penn. Bodyguards or even Penn himself might be up in her apartment. They could arrange an ambush at the stairs. That would be bad enough, but at least Manning and Smith would be able to see their attackers and fight back. There is no way to fight back if one is inside an elevator and the enemy severs the cables or drops grenades down the shaft. Manning always felt vulnerable in an elevator, and he rarely used one if he could use stairs instead.

The Phoenix pro and the disgruntled police lieutenant climbed the stairs to the third floor. They encountered no ambushers or booby traps. Smith glanced at Manning with an expression that seemed to say: Now don't you feel foolish? The Canadian ignored him, well aware that following the rules of caution and survival was never foolish even when it proved to be unnecessary.

"Do you want to check the door for trip wires and electrical traps rigged to the doorknob?" Smith snorted as they approached Inger's apartment. "Or do you think we can insert the key and unlock the door without being blown to bits or electrocuted?"

"You've got the key, pal," Manning said as he stepped to the side of the door near the hinges. He opened his jacket and slid his hand to the grips of the Walther P-5 semiautomatic pistol under his arm. "You might want to stand clear of the door after you knock . . . just in case."

"I think you blokes—" Smith began, but a scream from within the apartment interrupted him.

A woman shrieked from the opposite side of the door. Smith fumbled with the passkey in the lock. His fingers trembled slightly as he turned the knob and shoved the door open. Almost as an afterthought, he decided to take Manning's advice and ducked back to the doorway.

Manning entered the apartment, the Walther P-5 held in a two-handed grip, arms extended. The Canadian rapidly scanned the spacious front room of Inger's quarters. The decor was impressive. The white shag carpet was three inches thick and matched the long white sofa and armchairs. A glass-topped coffee table stood in front of the furniture, a black marble ashtray and a black-and-gold cigarette lighter on its polished surface. Modernistic paintings—also black-and-white—hung from the cream-colored walls. Inger had an expensive stereo system, a Sylvania color television set and a VCR built into an entertainment center. An ebony bar with a black leather counter stood between the front room and the dining table beyond.

However, Manning did not have much time to admire the setting. His attention quickly zeroed in on two struggling figures at one end of the sofa. The woman was a beautiful blonde with full breasts, a lean belly and long, shapely legs. The lovely limbs kicked wildly as a man dressed in a dirt-smeared white suit pinned the female to the floor. Her golden robe was open and the man straddled her chest, thighs jammed under her breasts. The beauty of her Nordic features was distorted by pain and terror. She no longer screamed as her assailant's dark fingers encircled her neck, his thumbs digging into her windpipe.

"My God!" Smith exclaimed, awkwardly drawing his snubnose Colt revolver from a belt holster.

Manning had already ascertained that the strangler appeared to be the only aggressor in the apartment. Manning reached the struggling pair in two strides. The male did not seem to notice. He remained fully absorbed in the task of throttling the woman. Manning heard an ugly liquid growl from the man as a strand of saliva dangled from his mouth onto the woman's naked breasts.

The Canadian warrior swung a hard kick to the ribs of the strangler. The powerful blow knocked the man from the woman, but he didn't relinquish his stranglehold on the woman. Her head bobbed limply with the motion, eyes open, tongue dangling loosely from her gaping mouth. She did not appear to be breathing.

Manning stomped a heel into the strangler's arm. The attacker's fingers mercifully loosened from around the woman's neck. The assailant looked up at Manning. No pain was evident in the mulatto's features; the eyes seemed glazed and immobile. With a start, Manning realized he had seen this man before.

It was Montgomery Penn.

Snarling like a beast, the gangster glared at Manning. He did not seem to recognize the Phoenix fighter, but he acknowledged the Canadian as an enemy. Manning pointed the muzzle of his Walther pistol directly at the hoodlum's face. Penn did not seem to care or even realize the gun presented a threat. Manning's stomach felt as if a cat had suddenly crawled inside it with its claws bared. He recognized the blank, emotionless expression on his opponent's face.

Penn had been transformed into a zombie.

As the gangster started to rise from the floor, Manning kicked the zombie in the jaw. Penn hurtled backward, crashed into the bar. His head struck the ebony base and bounced. Blood oozed from his mouth down his bruised chin and onto his filthy torn shirt.

Smith trained his revolver on the semiconscious man as Manning knelt by Inger's still form and touched the woman's neck. Her neck was marred by black-and-purple marks. Manning placed two fingers to her carotid artery. He found no pulse.

"Oh, God," Smith said, his breath ragged with tension as he held his revolver in both fists, aimed at Penn. "I don't believe this is really happening."

"You damn well better believe it," Manning snapped, risking a quick glimpse up at Smith. The cop was shaking so badly Manning thought he might rattle some bones loose. "The woman seems dead, but I'm gonna try to revive her with CPR. You keep Penn covered."

"*That's* Montgomery Penn?" Smith glared at the wild-eyed, gurgling beast clad in dirt-caked, tattered clothing.

"He was last night," Manning replied as he shoved his pistol into his belt and propped open Inger's mouth. "Not real sure what he is now."

Manning sealed his lips around the woman's mouth. Under different circumstances that would have appealed to the Canadian, but there was no life in Inger

Blomgren. There was nothing appealing about kissing a corpse. Tilting her head back to keep the neck straight, he pinched her nostrils shut and exhaled into her mouth. He took a breath and repeated the procedure, pressing an ear between her soft breasts, listening for a heartbeat.

He didn't hear one. Manning located her sternum and placed a palm on it. He locked the fingers of his other hand with it and pumped his arms. He was counting mentally, pressing hard with each count.

Penn started to get up; his jawbone was broken, so he moved sluggishly. He was not in pain, but he was tremendously dazed. The gangster-turned-zombie stared at Smith and Manning, his expression blank with a trace of confusion.

"You know CPR?" Manning asked Smith. "If you take over, I'll handle Penn...."

"That thing is coming at us!" Smith exclaimed, his revolver pointed at Penn's chest.

"Smith!" Manning shouted. "Hold your fire...."

The cop ignored the order and triggered his snub-nose revolver. The gun roared in the confined area. A slug smashed into Penn's chest; the zombie staggered along the bar. The cop fired two more rounds into Penn's shoulder blades.

"No!" Manning yelled, his voice lost amid the roar of more gunshots.

Smith emptied his weapon into Penn, who had slumped across a barstool. Staring at the bloodied body, the cop pulled the trigger twice more; the revolver clicked in his fist. The corpse collapsed to the floor, the chest ripped open by numerous wounds.

"I...I had to do it," Smith said, looking at the gun in his hand as if surprised to see it. "You saw. I had to...."

"It's done now," Manning replied, shaking his head as he climbed to his feet. "Can't change it."

"The woman?" Smith asked, gesturing toward the motionless female form with the revolver, which trembled in his shaky grasp.

"She's dead," Manning answered. "*Really* dead. Thyroid cartilage is crushed, so CPR won't do any good. She isn't breathing, there's no heartbeat, and she's probably brain-dead by now."

"God," Smith muttered, slowly returning his revolver to its holster. "What do we do now?"

"I don't know," the Phoenix commando said. "This sure looks like a dead end, and I don't have any idea of what's left for us to try."

**14**

"This looks like a charming place," David McCarter remarked as he glanced up at the legend above the tavern door. The Pirates' Lair was printed beneath a skull and crossbones with a fanged serpent slithering from a black eye socket. "Sure they'll let us in without reservations?"

"Just remember what I told you about this place," Rafael Encizo warned. "Just about everybody who comes here is involved in smuggling, drug trafficking, fencing stolen goods or some other criminal activity. They'll cut your throat and dump your corpse in the bay just to see what you've got in your pockets."

St. Ann's Bay did not seem a likely spot for hoodlums to choose for disposing of victims, but one would not expect to find a place like the Pirates' Lair near Ocho Rios, one of the most popular resort areas in Jamaica. As to the name, many tourists mistakenly think it is Spanish for "eight rivers," but it is actually a distortion of *chorreras*—which means "spouts." The reason for this is obvious at a glance. Several mountains are located in the region, and rivers flow through the limestone to form cascades of blue-and-white water. The coast by Ocho Rios features a series of water-falls, most notably the magnificent Dunn's River Falls.

Ocho Rios also offers several restaurants and hotels, including a couple that are remarkably inexpensive—less than thirty dollars a night. Even the surrounding villages of Oracabessa and Firefly are popular with tourists because they were formerly the respective vacation residences of Ian Fleming and Noel Coward.

However, the Pirates' Lair was located in a small fishing village that had never been a hangout for famous novelists or playwrights. Little more than a collection of shabby buildings and sheds, it was the sort of place tour guides warn tourists to avoid. Yet it was also the sort of place Todd Kevinson might flee to if he was running from a crime syndicate in Kingston.

Encizo, familiar with the Pirates' Lair from his previous visit to Jamaica, had been mildly surprised to learn the tavern still existed. Encizo had half expected it to have been blown to bits by rival gangs or shut down by the cops, but the Lair was still in business and apparently still frequented by underworld figures big and small.

After what had happened at the Palace of Madrid, Todd Kevinson realized his ass was on the line. The veteran black marketeer and smuggler would not stay in Kingston, and Spanish Town was out of the question. Encizo did not know all of Kevinson's haunts, but he figured that the Pirates' Lair was a likely spot for Kevinson to head. Perhaps they would find him there, perhaps not. If they did, there was a strong possibility the smuggler would want nothing to do with them.

"They dump many bodies in the bay?" McCarter inquired, speaking softly as they approached the Pirates' Lair.

"More than you'd guess," Encizo replied, tugging on the lapels of his navy peacoat, which concealed the H&K pistol in shoulder leather and the Cold Steel Tanto on his belt.

"Charming," McCarter muttered, swinging a knapsack over his shoulder. The Briton also wore a peacoat with his trusty Browning autoloader holstered under his arm.

"Just stay alert," Encizo warned. "A fella can get killed here, David."

"Sounds like my kind of place," the British ace said with a wolfish smile.

They entered the Pirates' Lair. A dense fog of cigar and pipe smoke filled the barroom. At one table, two Asian mulattoes were drinking a pitcher of beer. A large black man, dressed in cutoff jeans and a fishnet undershirt that displayed lots of muscular tattooed flesh, leaned against the bar, deliberating upon which beer-bottle cap to move on a checkerboard. The tattooed man was playing checkers with a heavyset mulatto behind the bar. Three black Jamaicans were talking in hushed whispers at another table.

Everyone in the barroom seemed to glance suspiciously at the two newcomers. Encizo stepped to the counter and nodded to the bartender, who exchanged glances with his tattooed friend. Mr. Tattoo jerked his head toward Encizo and McCarter. The bartender nodded and approached the new arrivals.

"What d'ya want?" he asked curtly, scratching his fat belly. The butt of a pistol protruded from his belt.

"Got any Myers rum?" Encizo asked, addressing the entire room in general and the bartender in particular.

"We got it, mon," the barman answered.

"Hey, paleface!" one of the black dudes across the room shouted at McCarter. "This ain't the kinda place you wants to be. Gets a little too dark for your kind in here."

"My heart's blacker than your skin, mate," McCarter growled as he placed his knapsack on the bar. "Just leave me be. We'll both be better off."

"Fuckin' Brit bastard..." the surly man began as he and his comrades started to rise from their chairs.

"Let it drop," the tattooed man said in a sharp tone without raising his voice. The men remained in their seats.

"I'll pour your drinks. Gulp them down fast and then get out," the bartender announced, reaching for a bottle of rum.

"We want twenty crates of Myers rum," Encizo declared. "And somebody who can deliver it to an address in Florida without running into the authorities along the way."

"I serve drinks," the bartender stated, placing a bottle of rum on the counter. "That's all I do, feller."

"Any of you fellas deal in selling and transportation of larger amounts of goods?" Encizo asked the others in the room.

"I think I smell a copper," an Asian mulatto commented, wrinkling his nose.

"Maybe you fellers came into the wrong place," Tattoo stated, displaying a mirthless grin. "We don't look for no trouble. We just do fishin' and dock work, mon. Best you go someplace else."

"That's not what we heard," McCarter stated, leaning on the bar with his arms folded across the counter. One hand rested under the knapsack.

"We heard a fella comes in here a lot who handles all sorts of special deliveries," Encizo remarked, taking a wad of bills from his pocket. He counted out one hundred Jamaican dollars and placed the money on the bar. "Whoever helps me find him will receive a reward for his cooperation."

"I might know him, mon," the bartender said, pouring rum into two glasses and gazing at the money with an expression similar to that of a starving man looking at a steak dinner.

"His name is Todd Kevinson," Encizo explained.

"Christ!" one of the black guys at the table exclaimed as he stood and reached inside his denim vest for whatever weapon he carried.

David McCarter had been half expecting something like that to happen. He yanked his M-10 machine pistol from the knapsack and aimed the compact Ingram blaster at the men at the table. The guy who was about to draw a weapon froze. One of his friends raised his hands. The third turned his back to Mc-Carter and slowly reached for something in his belt.

"Don't try it," the Briton warned. "Everybody put their hands in the air or I open fire *now*. This Ingram fires more than seven hundred rounds per minute. With thirty-two parabellums, I can shred the lot of you in about two seconds."

The three black dudes raised their hands. The bartender lowered a hand to the Largo pistol in his belt. Encizo coughed softly to get the guy's attention. The bartender glanced up and found himself staring into the muzzle of the Cuban's Heckler & Koch pistol.

"Two fingers," the Hispanic Phoenix pro instructed. "Use 'em to take the gun out slowly and place it on the bar."

The bartender nodded, his eyes as wide as if the lids had locked back. He slowly placed the pistol on the counter. Encizo shifted his attention from the bartender to the tattooed man, pointing his H&K pistol between them to effectively threaten both without favoring either. The Cuban grabbed the bartender's Largo and stuck it in his belt. Mr. Tattoo folded his musclar arms on his chest and calmly smiled at Encizo.

"You fellers are quick, mon," he remarked. "Don't figure you be coppers. What you want with Kevinson?"

"Just want to talk to him," Encizo answered, lowering his pistol. "Do you know where I can find him?"

"Maybe," Tattoo said with a shrug. "What's in it for me?"

Encizo did not trust him. Mr. Tattoo was too relaxed under the circumstances. Yet his stance was not as casual as it seemed. Encizo noticed Tattoo's knees were slightly bent, one foot forward. The guy was poised for attack, and Encizo recognized a fellow knife fighter when he saw one.

"See the money on the bar?" the Cuban inquired, tilting his head toward the cash he had placed there.

"What else?" Tattoo asked.

"I won't blow a bullet hole through your head," Encizo answered with an unpleasant smile that would have looked perfectly natural on a hungry tiger shark.

"That appeals to me, mon," the tattooed man assured him. He did not seem quite as confident as before.

"These blokes seem to know about Kevinson," McCarter commented, his Ingram still aimed at the three dudes at the table. "You blokes would rather talk to us than have me chop you off at the kneecaps. Wouldn't you?"

"Jesus," one of the men said fearfully.

"Hey, mon," an Asian mulatto began. "This ain't none of our business. We don' want nothin' to do with it. Okay?"

"We'll keep our mouths shut," his companion declared. "Just let us go..."

"Nobody gets hurt unless somebody gets stupid," Encizo promised. "But my friend is a little trigger-happy. He'd probably enjoy killing everybody in this room if somebody provokes him.''

"It's what I live for," McCarter replied with an exaggerated crazy-man smile. It was not too hard for the Briton to conjure up the expression.

"I doubt if you fellers are that good," the tattooed man snorted, slowly unfolding his arms to allow his hands to drop by his hips. "Really think you two could get all of us?''

"You want to find out?" the Cuban asked as he pulled back his jacket to reveal the Cold Steel Tanto sheathed on his belt. "You're ready to go for your blade. You're so eager to find out if you can take me, I can smell it.''

"You think that'll help you find Kevinson?" the tattooed man replied, moving a hand toward his hip pocket.

"Your friends will be eager to talk after they see what I do to you," Encizo answered.

"Shit!" Tattoo spit as his hand yanked a large switchblade knife from his pocket.

An eight-inch steel blade snapped into place. The tattooed thug lunged, knifepoint aimed at Encizo's belly. The Cuban drew his Tanto. Steel clashed as Encizo swept the heavy blade across his opponent's knife to deflect the attack.

A twist of the wrist altered the Cuban's knife stroke to slash the edge of his Tanto across the fist holding the switchblade. The sharp blade cut skin, muscle and bone. The Cold Steel weapon was a modern version of a samurai *tanto* fighting knife. It carved through the tattooed man's thumb and bisected it between the knuckles.

Tattoo screamed as his switchblade hit the floor. His thumb fell beside it. Blood spurted from the stump of the amputated digit. Encizo's left fist slammed into his opponent's jaw. The tattooed man staggered along the length of the bar, crimson still jetting from his mutilated hand. Encizo caught up with him and planted a knee in the guy's abdomen. Tattoo gasped and grabbed his bloodied hand with the uninjured other.

Encizo shoved him backward across the bar and placed the razor edge of his Tanto knife under Tattoo's chin. The hood trembled with fear and pain. All the toughness drained out of his features. He was no longer a confident knife artist waiting for a chance to slip his blade between a man's ribs for pocket money. He was just a frightened little crook with a knife at his throat.

"Where's Kevinson?" the Cuban hissed, his face less than an inch from Tattoo's nose. "Talk or I'll cut your head off and throw it in the bay so the fish can have your eyeballs for supper."

"In the basement!" the tattooed man said quickly, tears filling his eyes and sweat pouring from his brow. "He's hidin' out in the basement, for Christ's sake!"

"Get him," Encizo told the bartender. "Tell Todd Rafael wants to see him. Tell him if he tries to run we'll break his legs and take him anyway."

"Okay, mon," the bartender replied, nodding rapidly and heading for the back room.

"After you do that, call a doctor for your pal before he bleeds to death," Encizo added. "One of you other jokers go behind the bar and see if you can find some ice."

"One of you," McCarter told the two Asian mulattos. "Everybody else stays put."

Encizo removed the knife from Tattoo's throat. The hood slumped to the floor and landed on his backside. He clutched his mangled hand and tried to stop the blood; he did not look up at Encizo or the others.

"You fuckin' prick," he hissed, obviously talking to Encizo. "I'm gonna kill you for this."

"No fun to jump somebody who fights back?" the Cuban replied as he returned the Tanto to its belt sheath. "You're lucky this time, fella. A doctor can probably sew your thumb back on. While it's healing, you might think about what you're doing with your life. Next man you cross blades with might just kill you."

The bartender returned from the back room. A small, thin figure, with features that resembled an ebony rat with a nervous condition, stood beside him. Todd Kevinson held a Sterling submachine gun, but pointed the barrel at the ceiling. He did not look very happy to see Encizo and McCarter.

"What the hell do you want, Rafael?" Kevinson demanded. "I'm already a marked man. Ain't that bad enough? How the hell did you find me? How'd you know I'd be here?"

"We came to take you in for protective custody," Encizo answered. "We also have some more questions for you, Todd. Since Penn might have a contract on you, the safest place for you right now is with us."

"Sure," Kevinson snorted as he stepped around the bar. "You blew it last night, Rafael. You let Penn and the Haitians get away. Why should I go anywhere with you again?"

"Because we found you," Encizo replied. "If we can locate you this easy, Penn's people can find you just as easily, and they'll be a lot less gentle than we are."

"This is disgusting," Kevinson sighed as he lowered the Sterling to the floor. "You bastards are probably right. Let's go."

## 15

The Ruins might seem an unlikely name for a high-quality restaurant that has consistently received critical ranking of no less than three stars and often five stars for excellent food and atmosphere. Yet The Ruins is one of the finest outdoor restaurants in Jamaica. A forty-foot waterfall provides a breathtaking setting for the wooden deck dining sections. Tables are shaded by trees, and an Oriental footbridge extends from the patios.

All five men of Phoenix Force assembled at a table near the waterfall, where the rush of water helped cover their voices from unwanted eavesdroppers. Sergeant Della Walkins, Sergeant Bristol, Lieutenant Smith and Todd Kevinson were also at the table, and all were making casual chitchat about how lovely Ocho Rios was at that time of year. They gushed over Jamaican sites and how wonderful the Caribbean was. Finally, after they ordered and the waiter left, the group discussed its mission.

"I don't believe it," Kevinson muttered, gulping a glass of straight rum and ice. "I'm sittin' here with a bunch of coppers and whatever the hell you other blokes are. What the hell sort of outfit are you mixed up with, Rafael?''

"Just shut up and drink, Todd," Encizo replied. "As I recall, you were always pretty good at getting drunk."

"So long as somebody else is buyin'," the smuggler said. "I'm not sure whether I should be celebratin' or boozin' it up because I'm a condemned mon. You did say Montgomery Penn is dead, right?"

"Very dead," Manning confirmed, raising a cup of black coffee to his lips. "Deadeye Smith saw to that."

"Damn it, I acted in self-defense," Lieutenant Smith snapped as he banged a fist on the table near his double Scotch and water. "And you know it!"

"Keep your voice down," Yakov Katzenelenbogen warned, glancing around The Ruins. "This is a public place and not far from the Americana or the Sheraton Hotel. We don't need to share this conversation with any tourists."

"I was surprised you managed to get reservations here," Della remarked. "But I see the place isn't as crowded as usual. Tourism has gone down, and business suffers when that happens."

"That doesn't seem very important right now," Smith complained. "I don't appreciate goddamn Yank foreigners suggesting I killed a man without good reason."

"Sort of hard to claim self-defense when there is a case of overkill," Calvin James said with a shrug. "Even if the guy was a zombie."

"Go easy on him, mate," David McCarter urged with mock sympathy for Smith's plight. "After all, the lieutenant was under a lot of stress. Bristol here knows about that. He shot a fella once under similar circumstances. Personally, I think it's easier to understand pulling a trigger as a reflex action because somebody took a shot at you, but I'm sure Smith will convince the investigation of the shooting that his actions were justified."

"Yes," Bristol began, surprised by the support he received from the Phoenix commandos. "I suppose so."

"An investigation would probably be contrary to the national security of Jamaica and the security of this mission," Katz remarked, offering Smith a chance to save face. "I don't see that anything is to be gained by raking over the details of either incident. No innocent persons were harmed due to either shooting, although both are certainly regrettable."

"I imagine that would be for the best," Smith agreed, his tone revealing both a trace of resentment and relief at Katz's suggestion.

"Am I missin' some information here?" Kevinson inquired.

"Yeah," Encizo told him. "And let's keep it that way."

"What is this slimy little smuggler doing here?" Bristol asked, watching Kevinson gulp down his drink. "Since Penn is dead, this toad can't lead us to him. Why not let him crawl back under his rock so we can get back to work?"

"Be okay with me, mon," Kevinson said with a sniffle. "I would have been happy to stay at the Pirates' Lair, but Rafael and his buddy came lookin' for me. After I eat I'll crawl back under my rock and leave this gunplay nonsense to you blokes...."

"Not yet," Encizo declared. "Penn's dead, and you know more about his syndicate than anyone we've been able to question so far."

"I was never part of his gang, for crissake," the smuggler said. "By the way, I need another drink."

"Did you ever hear of Haldren or Griswald?" Calvin James asked, checking a notepad to be certain of the names.

"Penn's top lieutenants in the syndicate," Kevinson answered. "Not sure where you'd find 'em."

"Haldren is back in Kingston," James explained, sipping a tall glass of beer. "He's in the city morgue. We paid him a visit just before we left Kingston to meet you guys here. Jonathan Haldren was fished out of the water near Port Royal around noon today, but the local cops didn't know who he was until they ran a check on his fingerprints. Lucky they called Kingston for the records. Haldren apparently had an accident while snorkeling. Probable cause of death is listed as drowning."

"No idea what happened to Griswald?" Gary Manning asked.

"Colonel Wells sent some agents to Griswald's home in Mandeville," Della Walkins explained. "Griswald's wife said she hadn't heard from him since he went off to meet with some chums at the Manchester Club this morning. However, Arthur Griswald isn't a member of the club, and they have no idea who he is or where he might be.''

"Mandeville?" Kevinson frowned. ''I thought Griswald lived in Mo' Bay.''

"Mo' Bay?" McCarter raised his eyebrows. "You mean Montego Bay?''

"Native Jamaicans usually call it Mo' Bay," Encizo told his British partner. "Are you sure about Griswald and Montego Bay, Todd?''

"I know he used to run some smugglin' operations outta Mo' Bay 'cause I handled a boat for him on a couple occasions," Kevinson confirmed. "Griswald was sort of Penn's top boy when it came to smugglin' operations. He was co-owner of a number of boats in Mo' Bay. Fishin' vessels, speedboats, even a yacht or two.''

"Did you come across anything about that when you checked out Griswald's records?" Katz asked, turning to Della.

"No," the lady cop answered. "Griswald has been connected with Penn for years, but no one was ever able to prove he was guilty of anything. He even stood trial on three occasions. Twice for suspicion of smuggling and once for conspiracy to commit murder. Witnesses either refused to testify or disappeared. The previous charges of smuggling were supposed to have taken place around Port Royal and Long Bay. I don't think anyone ever suspected Griswald was involved in any smuggling operations in Montego Bay.''

"Think it's worth looking into?" Bristol inquired.

"I don't know what else to do under the circumstances," Katz admitted. The Israeli was about to light a cigarette when two waiters approached with their meals.

Everyone except Bristol and Smith had ordered the lotus-lily lobster—a gourmet legend at The Ruins. This was the first meal in a quality restaurant any of the men of Phoenix Force had been able to enjoy since their arrival in Jamaica. They intended to make the most of the opportunity. Della Walkins and Todd Kevinson had also taken advantage of the chance to eat a classic lobster dinner they would not ordinarily have been able to afford.

Bristol and Smith had ordered Chinese dishes. The Ruins has a reputation for having the finest Chinese food in Jamaica—if not the entire Caribbean. They waited for the waiters to leave before continuing the conversation.

"I have an idea that might be worth checking out," Calvin James announced. "Cercueil has been getting his zombies by abducting winos and baking their brains with drugs and electrical torture...."

"Most of them had probably already lost their willpower from years of hitting the bottle," Smith remarked.

"Maybe," James said with a shrug, "but don't forget Montgomery Penn was zombified, too. They managed that in less than eight hours. Cercueil's zombie-makers must be getting pretty good at turning human beings into robot-slaves."

"Sweet Jesus," Bristol whispered. "You mean those damn Haitians can turn *anyone* into a zombie?"

"Possibly," James answered. "If they had enough time. In Penn's case, Cercueil obviously decided the guy was a liability. So his people did a special job on Penn. My guess is the autopsy will reveal Penn received an extra dose of everything—drugs, electrical shock and maybe a few other nasty tricks. Still, don't be too impressed. Penn was a prick to begin with. Turning an amoral gangster into a mindless killer isn't exactly transforming St. Francis into Jack the Ripper."

"Why didn't they just kill him?" Kevinson asked.

"This doesn't concern you," Encizo told him, passing a bottle of white wine to the smuggler. "Just get drunk like a good fellow, okay?"

"I can do that," Kevinson said, and poured himself a drink.

"He has a good question," Smith pointed out. "Killing Penn would have been easier. Why turn him into a zombie and force him to kill his mistress?"

"Because it accomplished three goals simultaneously," Katz explained. "Whatever Penn knew about Cercueil's activities was wiped away forever when they altered his brain to make him a zombie. Whatever his mistress knew was taken care of when Penn killed her. Finally, the murder of Inger isn't a mystery. Officially, Penn murdered her. He was an underworld figure, and no one will be too surprised to hear a gangster strangled his girlfriend and was later shot to death by the police. Cercueil knows damn good and well we don't intend to tell the public Penn was a zombie. That would cause more problems among the obeah cults and other voodoo-related groups. More confusion, fear and stronger belief in Cercueil's 'mystical powers.' We'll cover up the facts, and our Ton Ton Macoute opponents know it."

"You think Wells will agree to that?" Bristol asked.

"Absolutely," Katz assured him. "The governor-general's office doesn't want this sort of thing getting out. Of course, there will always be rumors, but no one will be able to prove anything. Unless Cercueil's side wins."

"You think that's possible?" Smith asked with a frown.

"Of course it is," the Phoenix Force commander replied. "Now, what were you saying about the winos, Mr. Johnson?"

"Oh, yeah," James said, nearly forgetting his alias. "It occurred to me that the bad guys must be hunting for suitable burned-out bums to turn into a fresh batch of zombies after we wiped out their supply at de Madrid's place. Maybe we can catch them when they try to round up some fresh replacements."

"And maybe Cercueil has a hundred extra zombies already locked away elsewhere on the island," Gary Manning remarked, shaking his head grimly. "Or the son of a bitch may have already fled the country after zombifying Penn and any of his lieutenants who might have known the details of the Haitian's scheme here in Jamaica."

"Still worth checking out," James insisted. "How about me looking into that possibility while you check out Griswald's activities in Montego Bay?"

"I don't want you doing that on your own," Katz declared. "You'll need backup."

"He'll get it," Bristol announced. "Most of the worse slum areas are located in or near Kingston. I'm familiar with them. I'll back him up. With extra men, of course."

"I hope you know what you're doing," Katz said. "If anything goes wrong and Cercueil's people get the upper hand, you might be lucky if they *just* kill you."

## 16

The Jamaican Crafts Market in Kingston offers tourists a chance to purchase hundreds of unusual curios, works of art and native crafts unavailable anywhere else on the island, and prices are often lower at the market than at other places in Jamaica. One can buy almost anything at the market. In fact, the area has a reputation as a hustlers' hangout. Dope dealers and black marketeers frequently hit on customers trying to enter the market.

Near the Crafts Market, by the waterfront, a number of storage houses and sheds served as a congregation point for men who had nothing to sell and seldom any money to buy. They were losers in the game of life. Each man had a different story, but all the endings were the same. Some told of losing jobs or wives, others of associates who had conspired to ruin their big dreams, still others of how the government had loused up their businesses. All had eventually turned to drink to help numb the pain and frustration. Alcohol helped them forget the tragedies, real or imagined, that had led to their downfalls. Eventually most would even forget what had caused them to crawl into a bottle to escape the disappointments and hardships of life.

The winos gathered along the waterfront to warm themselves around small fires. They traded with one another. None of them had much, but they spent the daylight hours trying to find food, shelter, warmth, discarded cigarette butts, maybe a few coins. They traded tobacco for food, old newspapers for chewing gum, pieces of string for pieces of adhesive tape.

As hobos, they had learned unique survival skills. They used newspaper to line clothing for warmth, and fashioned it into pillows and crude blankets. String replaced broken shoelaces or missing belts. Bits of tape served as patches for torn or threadbare clothing. Cardboard was good for temporarily mending holes in shoes. An old poster became a rain shield. The bums found a use for almost everything they came across.

Though many spent a lot of time begging, few ever managed to collect enough money to buy a bottle of cheap wine or rotgut whiskey or rum without pooling their financial gains with several of their pals. Together they usually had enough for a bottle. This was generally justified as "something to keep the chill away." The winos also shared food in a similar manner. They generally dined on scraps of meat, vegetables, catsup and other items boiled in a tin can to form a cross between garbage and soup.

They were a strange group with a particular set of values and code of conduct. Many people thought they lived like animals, yet hobos formed friendships, cooperated with one another, and seldom fought among themselves. They were also very suspicious of strangers.

The two newcomers who approached the five-man "family" of hobos were dressed in shabby clothing, old boots and battered hats with shapeless brims. One man wore a wrinkled raincoat with a torn pocket. Both men were tall, black, and appeared to be less than thirty-five years old.

The hobos sensed something was wrong about the pair. Although their senses had been dulled by years of abuse and the loss of millions of brain cells to the alcohol-rot, they somehow understood that these two were different. The strangers' clothes were wrinkled and ill-treated, but the garments did not look dirty enough. But the bums' own clothes smelled so badly they would have been hard-pressed to recognize a stench other than their own.

The strangers did not move quite like real winos. Were they new to the harsh world of the alleys, piers and hobo jungles? Maybe they had just recently hit bottom. Or maybe they were trouble. Sometimes new guys steal, even kill for enough pennies to buy a bottle of cheap rotgut. Every bum had been assaulted at one time or another; some carried scars as permanent reminders. They had all seen men die in this manner. Generally, two or more younger, stronger bastards would attack an older, weaker hobo and either beat him to death or cut him open.

However, this was an extraordinary circumstance, for not only did the two strangers not appear to be threatening, but one of them carried a familiar and much-sought-after object in a brown paper bag. The bottle was enough to convince the hobos to let the newcomers get closer.

"Yo' fellers wants to join us?" Sheldon, the unofficial leader of the hobo clan, offered with a toothless grin. "Could maybe trade you for somethin'. Especially if you be willin' to share what yo' got in dat bag."

"Sure, mon," Calvin James replied, handing the bottle to Sheldon. "Nice jus' to be warmed by yo' fire. Kinda chilled tonight, ain't it so?"

"Yo' sure right 'bout that, mon," Sheldon agreed as he stripped away the bag to examine the bottle. He licked his lips when he discovered it to be almost full of Myers rum. "Dis is purely a bea-*yoo*-tiful sight. Mighty good again' the chill."

"I gots a little ganja," another hobo declared, taking several partially smoked cigarette butts from a pocket. "Least I thinks one of dese is ganja."

"Never liked it much no way," Sergeant Bristol replied with an exaggerated shrug. He had to bite his tongue when the guy mentioned "ganja"—Jamaican slang for marijuana. "Thanks, but you keep it, mon. Is okay?"

"Fockin' fog comin' in tonight," Sheldon observed, watching the gray mist floating across the bay. "Mighty glad yo' sharin' the bottle, brother. Where yo' come from, mon?"

"We been up 'round Run'way Bay till couple days 'go," James answered. "Fockin' tourists ain't goin' there much these days. Like a ghost town up there now."

"Tourists ain't here much, neither," a hobo announced after taking a long swallow of rum. "Lots a' bad things been happenin' all 'round island. Bad times, mon. Real bad."

"Yo' blokes do good to stay with us tonight," Sheldon offered. His concern for their safety seemed genuine. "Not be wise to go 'round by yo'selves after dark no more."

"Heard rumors folks been sorta disappearin'," James remarked as he squatted by the fire. "Folks like us what don't live in no houses."

"Ain't jus' rumors," a scrawny little bum with a thick gray beard stated grimly. "I seen 'em get a bloke last week, maybe the week afore that. Memory ain't so good no more. Two fellers jus' grabbed this bloke an' stuffed 'im in a truck. I seen that and I knows what I seen, mon. Lucky they didn't get me, too."

"Christ Jesus," Bristol said, shaking his head. "Was they coppers what done this?"

"I don't thinks they was," the skinny bum replied, taking the bottle from a companion. "They's bad fellers. That be for sure. You gents want a swig?"

"Later," James assured him. "Yo' gettin' me kinda scared now. What these fellers want with us? We ain't got no money or nothin'."

"Is obeah men what's doin' it," the scrawny man answered. "They left a mark to warn us off. Chicken leg cut off with a twig of hemlock in its claws. Seen it afore. Obeah. Voodoo. Best to stay far 'ways from that, mon.''

"Best we sticks together, too," Sheldon added.

"Makes sense to me," James agreed.

Just then the white beams of two headlights appeared along the harbor, cutting through the dense fog. The hobos exchanged nervous glances as the lights approached. Sheldon grabbed the tin can on the fire and poured some watery soup on the flames to put them out.

"Maybe we better hide," someone suggested.

"Best be safe," the clan leader agreed as the sound of the engine became louder. "Probably nothin', but I reckon we're all a bit spooked what with all's been goin' on...."

A large dark gray vehicle, a truck, rolled into view, blending into the fog-laced darkness like a chameleon on a tree branch. The lights glared into the faces of the hobos as the truck came to a halt. Doors opened, and two men emerged from the rig.

"I think we best be outta here, mon!" Sheldon announced as he quickly shuffled away.

The others followed, James and Bristol at the rear, moving slower than the rest. They were, of course, only pretending to flee. They hoped the strangers in the lorry would prove to be connected with Cercueil's outfit, and they did not really want to escape or allow the men from the truck to get away. Yet if they were to trap the abductors, the two undercover men had to appear to be a pair of frightened and half-incapacitated hobos, like Sheldon and his friends.

James and Bristol jogged behind the winos, imitating their awkward, uncoordinated gait. James glanced over his shoulder. The headlights nearly blinded him as the truck creeped forward. Two human shapes moved in the white glare. The enemy was chasing them. James was not certain if the pursuers carried weapons, but he knew they would not fire. Cercueil needed live bodies to turn into zombies.

"Stop right there, ya rum-soaked scum!" a man ordered, stepping from behind a stack of crates. He wore white duck trousers, a blue T-shirt and a denim jacket. The man aimed a .12-gauge pump shotgun with a cut-down barrel at the hobos.

"We ain't done nothin'," Sheldon declared, raising his hands above his head. "We gots nothin' worth stealin'—"

"Shut up!" the man with the shotgun snapped. "Open your mouth again and I'll splatter you all over the dock."

The truck and two other hoodlums approached the group. The driver, sticking his head out the window, called out to his companions; one of them jogged over and spoke with him. Meanwhile, the shotgunner kept the hobos covered.

James and Bristol held their hands at shoulder level and waited. They hoped the backup team was in position and the radio transmitters hidden in their clothing had informed the team that they were in trouble.

"Hey, those guns ain't necessary," James declared, speaking for the transmitter to make the situation clear to the backup team...providing somebody was listening to the radio receiver.

"Didn't you hear what I told that other scumbum?" the shotgun man snapped, gesturing at James with his weapon. "That goes for you, too, puke-eater. Open your mouth again and you'll be eatin' buckshot."

"Okay," one of the hoods announced. "Get in the truck. We ain't got all night."

"You ain't gots no right to—" the scrawny hobo began.

A hoodlum stepped forward and quickly rammed the muzzle of a pistol into the bum's slim waist. The hobo doubled up with a gasp and received a knee under his jaw. His head snapped back, his knees buckled and he collapsed to the boardwalk.

"Disgusting lump of shit," the thug growled as he kicked the fallen man in the ribs.

"That's enough!" Bristol snapped, stepping forward as if to protect the battered wino.

The thug grabbed Bristol's tattered jacket by the lapel, yanked him forward, and jammed the muzzle of his pistol under the cop's jaw. James clenched his teeth and stifled a curse. The Phoenix pro slowly lowered his hands and held his breath. Bristol was not acting like a rummy hobo, and the three hoods would become suspicious if they realized he was not what he appeared to be.

"You reckon you're tough, boy?" the thug demanded as he dug the pistol into the hollow of Bristol's jaw. "Ain't nobody tougher than a bullet."

"Okay..." Bristol said through clenched teeth as the pressure of the gun under his jaw increased. "I...I'm sorry, mon."

"What the fuck is this?" the hood said with a start, noticing and then touching something hard beneath Bristol's jacket. "Hey, this bastard's packin' heat!"

"What?" the shotgunner eyed the hobos with sudden concern. "You sure about that, Walt?"

"I'm gonna make sure," the pistol-toting hood stated. With his pistol still braced under Bristol's jaw, he slid his free hand inside the cop's jacket. "Don't move or I'll blow your head off."

Bristol stood rigid while the thug eased the .38 Colt snubgun from the holster under his arm. The thug named Walt smiled as he held the revolver in one hand, the pistol in his other hand pressed under Bristol's jawbone. He waved the cop's own gun in front of his face, taunting him with the weapon.

"Looks like we found us an undercover copper," he remarked. "Bet one or two of these other bastards are badge-boys, too."

"We'd better get the hell outta here," the shotgun man said nervously. "This smells like a goddamn setup."

"Yeah," Walt hissed, his voice filled with hate. "But this fuckin' cop ain't goin' anywhere 'cept to hell!"

*Jesus,* Calvin James thought, his stomach knotting into an icy fist. *That bastard is going to kill Bristol!*

The Phoenix commando's hand whipped back his dirt-smeared raincoat, found the Smith & Wesson

Model 76 that hung from a shoulder strap. His fist closed on the grip of the compact machine pistol, finger slipping into the trigger guard. James moved as fast as he could, realizing it might not be fast enough to save Sergeant Bristol.

The Kingston cop, also realizing Walt was about to pull the trigger, knew there was not enough time for him to safely jerk away from the pistol at his jaw; the hood would almost certainly shoot him before he could get clear. Sergeant Bristol made a decision: the last he would ever make, but still the correct choice under the circumstances.

Bristol moved with a speed born of desperation. He grabbed the snubnose revolver—the Colt—in Walt's left fist, and shoved the muzzle toward the thug's startled face. With his thumb he pressed on Walt's trigger finger.

Panicking, the hoodlum fired the pistol that was lodged in the hollow of Bristol's jaw. Instantaneously, the slug tore through Bristol's head and burst through the roof of his mouth. In the last moment of his life, the police sergeant had increased the pressure of his thumb on Walt's trigger finger, forcing him to fire the other revolver. It was the dying man's final wish.

The snubnose Colt—Bristol's weapon—exploded. A 132-grain copper-jacketed slug smashed into Walt's cheek below the left eye. Orbital bone cracked, and Walt's eyeball sprang from its socket. The bullet burned a path of destruction through the killer's skull and exited at the back of his head.

Bristol and Walt dropped simultaneously to the boardwalk.

James raised his S&W M-76 as the gunman near the truck was just swinging his Star PD toward the Phoenix pro. James triggered first. Three 9 mm slugs blasted into the hoodlum's chest. The impact hurled the body backward into the hood of the truck, and it slumped lifeless to the ground. Bloodstained, one of the headlights shone red.

Now the thug with the shotgun opened fire. He did not bother to aim, and simply blasted a load of buckshot into the group of hobos. A man next to Sheldon went down as if yanked to the plankwalk by invisible wires, his upper torso smashed and bloodied by double-O buckshot. Sheldon cried out and spun around from the force of three stray pellets that ripped into his left arm. Blood oozed from punctured skin and pulped muscle.

James swung his Smith & Wesson blaster toward the shotgunner as the killer was working the pump, preparing to fire another 12-gauge shell. The Phoenix warrior squeezed the trigger of his M-76 and pumped two parabellums into the hood's stomach. James continued to fire as the barrel rose, cutting a line of bullet holes through his opponent's chest, neck and throat. The shotgun tumbled away. The body of the gunman hit the boards with a liquid thud.

Panicked, the driver of the truck put the vehicle in reverse and tried to back away from the carnage. Dropping to one knee, James trained his machine pistol on the front tires of the rig. Half a dozen 9 mm rounds slashed into rubber. Bullets sang sourly against the metal hubs of the tires. The driver fought the wheel as his vehicle skidded across the pier. The last few rounds of the M-76 punctured the radiator. A bullet snapped the hood catch, and the hood popped up to block the windshield.

The truck swung into a crazy zigzag pattern. Virtually blinded and terrified, the driver steered to the right, then swung far left. Too far left. The truck rolled awkwardly to the edge of the pier. The driver jumped from the vehicle a moment before it tumbled over the brink. Slipping on the damp surface, he landed hard on a hip as the truck fell in the bay. Water splashed up and drenched the dazed hoodlum.

Calvin James scooped up the discarded Star PD and approached the surviving outlaw, who beseeched him, with eyes filled with pain and fear. Still lying on his back, the thug extended his arms high to show his hands were empty.

"Don't shoot, mon!" he cried, his voice strained by tension and pain. "My leg's busted! I give up! Okay?"

"Just shut up," James ordered, stepping over the lifeless shape of Sergeant Bristol. "I don't wanta hear you talk right now. I'm real fuckin' mad and it won't take much to convince me to kick your ass into the bay. So shut your mouth!"

Two cars rolled across the boardwalk, and several well-armed police officers appeared among the crates and storage buildings. From one of the autos stepped Lieutenant Smith and Della Walkins. The hobos cowered beside the corpse of their mutilated friend.

One of them wept; fear, sorrow and relief were expressed as a series of pitiful wails.

"Cal," Della said breathlessly as she ran to the Phoenix Force veteran. "Are you all right?"

"Bristol's dead," James replied. He watched two policemen approach the injured truck driver. James glanced down at the Star pistol in his fist. "They killed him right in front of me. I couldn't stop 'em!"

"God, Cal," Della said softly, placing a hand on his arm. "I'm sorry."

"I think we've got them all," Smith began, walking toward James. "How many were there, Johnson?"

"Where the hell were you?" James demanded, his eyes bright with anger. "You fuckers should have closed in the second you knew we were in trouble...."

"The radio receiver didn't work," Smith answered, his tone apologetic. "I think the fog screwed it up somehow. We didn't know you were in trouble until we heard the shots."

"Hell," James rasped. He nearly hurled the Star PD into the bay, but realized that would be a stupid gesture. He put the safety on and stuck the pistol in his belt. "What kind of shoddy equipment were you using? Bristol and I put our asses on the line and you're listening in with some piece of shit that can't even operate when the fog rolls in! Bristol's dead because of that fuckup...."

"I know," Smith said in a firm voice. "He was a good man. A fine police officer and a brave man. I wish I'd told him that before. Now it's too late."

"These guys were workin' for Cercueil, man," James said grimly. "We're gonna get that Haitian son of a bitch, Smith. I don't care what you or Wells think, or if we have to tear this island apart. We're gonna find Cercueil."

"Damn right we will," Smith agreed.

"And when we find him," James continued, stabbing a finger in the air, "I want him. Don't count on him standing trial, 'cause I'm gonna take care of his ass myself."

**17**

"The dude we nailed at the waterfront squealed like a stuck pig," Calvin James told the others the next day when he joined them on the beach at Jack Tar Village, a popular Montego Bay resort. "He admitted he was working for Cercueil. The guy was a street soldier for Penn's syndicate. Griswald's now the official leader of the outfit, but Cercueil's really calling the shots."

"Yeah," Gary Manning remarked, glancing at the morning sun above the beautiful Caribbean. "We know. Griswald was arrested last night. He was running his boat business under a phony name. We seized his records and spent most of the night going over them."

"Find anything interesting?" James asked, noticing several young women in bikinis lying on blankets. James could not enjoy their beauty. The image of Bristol's corpse was still too vivid in his mind.

"Very interesting," Yakov Katzenelenbogen replied. The Israeli sat in a folding chair with a hand towel draped over his prosthesis and a glass of iced tea in his left hand. "A sixty-foot motorboat was sold to a 'Morris Coffin' last month. Unless this is one hell of

a coincidence, I'd say we've located Maurice Cercueil . . . or the fellow who has assumed his identity."

"So where do we find this boat?" James asked eagerly.

"Don't worry," Encizo assured him. The Cuban
raised a glass of iced tea to his face and tapped the rim
against his dark sunglasses. "The mysterious Mr.
Coffin purchased a vessel called *Witchcraft*. It's been
floating around the bay off the coast for the last three
weeks. There aren't very many boats that size around
here, and most of them are commercial fishing vessels or passenger boats connected with tour companies. It won't be hard to find *Witchcraft*."

"Might be harder than you think, amigo," James
told him. "The stool pigeon told us Cercueil is getting ready to haul ass. He wants more winos turned
into zombies so he can turn them loose on more or less
indiscriminate targets. The dude didn't know too
many details about the plan, but he did tell us the
zombies were gonna be released in Kingston and the
targets would probably be native Jamaicans."

"That's a switch," David McCarter commented,
sipping a frosted glass of Coke as he watched a girl
remove the top of her bikini to sunbathe. The sight did
not interest him as much as it would have under different circumstances. "We were sent here because
Americans were being killed."

"I'm sure Cercueil has figured that out," Katz remarked, taking a pack of Camels from his shirt
pocket. "After all, if Jamaicans are suddenly the victims of zombies and perhaps other voodoo-related

causes, it would appear we were barking up the wrong conspiratorial tree. Soon the Jamaican government would insist we go home, and the President would have little choice but to agree to recall us.''

"Which would discredit our theories about Cercueil's plot to eventually take over Jamaica,'' Manning added. "In fact, if Cercueil gets away and the zombie attacks continue, the authorities may eventually decide he was never involved.''

"Yeah," Encizo said with a cynical snort. "Governments like nice simple explanations that let them off the hook. Everybody would be perfectly happy to blame all the murders and violence that have occurred here on a plain old crime wave. The zombies would be explained away as just crazed junkies on some sort of supercharged PCP. Everything else would be dismissed as gang warfare. The cops will be instructed to assure the public that the threat is over and all the bad guys are either dead or in jail.''

"Then everybody pretends nothing ever happened and Cercueil gets away?" James shook his head. "That ain't good enough.''

"He hasn't gotten away yet," Katz declared, "and he isn't going to. Until now we've been concentrating our activities in the Kingston area and Spanish Town. Now we know Cercueil has actually been in and around Montego Bay. Even if the Haitians flee to another island, they'll be stopped. We've already contacted Colonel Wells, and he's alerted the coastal patrols of the Cayman Islands, the Bahamas and the Dominican Republic. Although it's pretty unlikely

Cercueil would head for either Haiti or Cuba, those islands have been contacted as well. If he's floating around on the *Witchcraft*, he'll find nothing but dead ends."

"You guys did this even before I told you what we learned from the flunky the Kingston cops caught last night?" James asked, surprised. He smiled thinly and shrugged. "Hell, I should have figured you'd cover every possibility."

"Well, we're not going to let some coast-guard blokes get those bastards," David McCarter stated. "I don't think the patrol boats would try to arrest Cercueil and his crew, but they've been instructed to keep the *Witchcraft* from attaining sanctuary. They've also been warned that the Haitians are to be regarded as armed and extremely dangerous. If the *Witchcraft* tries to break through a patrol blockade, they'll blow it out of the water."

"So Cercueil and friends will be ours unless they force the patrols to blow them away," James said with a nod. "If we can find them before the *Witchcraft* turns around and heads for the Panama Canal."

"They'd find patrols waiting there, too," Katz replied. "But Wells suspects—and I agree—Cercueil will probably head for the Cayman Islands. Haiti or Cuba might be closer, but Cercueil obviously doesn't want to return to Haiti, and heading for a Communist country wouldn't appeal to him, either. Cayman Islands seem the most likely choice."

"What the hell are we waiting for?" James asked. "Let's go find those scumbags."

"We're waiting for a helicopter to arrive from Kingston," Encizo explained, placing a hand on James's shoulder. "And we're also waiting for some other special equipment that will arrive with the chopper. Don't worry, Cal."

"I just want Cercueil," James declared.

"Taking this sort of personal, aren't you?" Manning said with a frown. "This isn't a vendetta, Cal. If you let your anger get the better of your judgment, you could put us all in a bind."

"May I remind all of you that we need to take Cercueil or at least one of his top people alive?" Katz announced. "The police and the governor-general's office still need evidence to round up and arrest individuals still in Jamaica who conspired with Cercueil. Besides, we're not in the revenge business. Phoenix Force gets to bend a lot of laws and occasionally breaks a few, but we don't have a right to carry out impromptu executions."

"I'm not so sure that's wrong in the case of Cercueil and his bunch," James muttered.

"You may be right, Cal," Katz said with a nod. "But the notion that people don't have a right to a trial—isn't that the same mentality police death squads have exhibited in the past? The Nazis in Europe? SAVAK in Iran under the Shah? The NKVD under Stalin?"

"Or the guys in the white sheets with the pointed hats who lynch blacks?" Encizo added.

"Ouch." James winced at Encizo's remark. "I see what you mean. The goddamn Ton Ton Macoute was notorious for that sort of shit, as well. Here I'm talkin' about using the same tactics that helped make Cercueil into a monster."

"You didn't really mean it," Manning told his partner. "Bristol was killed in front of you. You're still upset about that. Cercueil has been responsible for a lot of death and suffering, but Bristol was the first victim any of us really knew. Maybe that shouldn't make a difference, but it does."

"Funny," James mused, gazing at the crystal-blue water of the Caribbean without really seeing it. "I didn't like Bristol when we first met. Turned out to be a pretty good guy after all, even if he was a jerk at times."

"Isn't everyone?" Katz asked with a kindly smile. "We got to know Bristol's good points and some of his negative personality traits. You don't find perfection among human beings, although no one is entirely evil, either. Maybe that's why Bristol's death affected you so much, Cal. You realized he was indeed a human being."

"Sometimes it bothers me that we find ourselves thinking of people as either sharply on our side or sharply on the other side," Gary Manning remarked. "We tend to regard our enemies as simply targets in a firefight. Half the time we don't really get to know the people on 'our side.' Yet everyone on both sides is still human. Sometimes I think we forget that."

"Oh, God," McCarter snorted. "You think blokes like Cercueil worry about this sort of thing? They're the ones who victimize innocent people. As far as I'm concerned, that's the big difference between them and us. That's why I don't fret about what we do. None of us ever killed a bloke without a damn good reason. That's enough morality for me."

"This is scary," Manning said with mock concern. "David said something that seemed to make sense. Has the world turned upside down?"

"You're about as funny as a rubber crutch," McCarter growled in reply.

"Gentlemen," Katz cut them off before the argument could escalate. "We still have to discuss strategy for handling the *Witchcraft* when we locate it. Cercueil and his lot aren't the type to just toss their weapons into the water and surrender."

PIERRE MAZARIN CERCUEIL SAT at his desk in his office-cabin aboard the *Witchcraft*. His black silk top hat hung on a wall peg, and his black suit jacket was draped over the back of his chair. Cercueil had loosened the necktie and unbuttoned the white shirt at his throat. The Baron Samedi costume was not the most comfortable choice of apparel.

The Ton Ton Macoute veteran was sorting through file folders. Cercueil did not intend to keep any records that were not essential for continuing his operations. The files on Montgomery Penn and other dead Jamaican hoodlums were no longer useful and might even be used as evidence against Cercueil if the authorities searched the boat. He dumped them into a wastebasket to be destroyed before they reached the Cayman Islands.

Cercueil might still need some contacts in Jamaica. He had spared Griswald for that reason. Griswald would take over Penn's syndicate, although Cercueil doubted the crime network would last long under Griswald's leadership. No matter. There would always be more criminals who could be enlisted to further Cercueil's cause. Greedy, selfish men who could be lured into conspiracy by bribes and promises of wealth and power.

The Haitian did not allow himself to dwell on the setback to his plan in Jamaica. Cercueil had suffered lesser setbacks before, and he had never given up. Too much time and money had been invested in his plan to eventually control all the islands of the Caribbean—with the probable exception of Cuba—with the aid of his sinister Ton Ton Macoute. He could not stop even if he wanted to, and Cercueil still believed in what he was doing. The island nations, he believed, would never be more than tourist playgrounds or dependencies of European countries unless the Ton Ton Macoute seized power and united the Caribbean under a strong central government.

Cercueil would continue his schemes when he reached the Cayman Islands. Assisting him would be Louis de Broglie, who was still his right-hand man, and several other passengers aboard the *Witchcraft*, including about a dozen strong-arms, two chemists and a former Port-au-Prince physician who helped Cercueil administer poisons, drugs and brainwashing techniques necessary to the formation of zombies. The experiment with Montgomery Penn proved the process could be successful applied to individuals other than skid-row winos. Perhaps they could eventually perfect the techniques to control a subject without destroying the person's mind. The prospect offered limitless possibilities.

"Pierre!" De Broglie's voice at the door was accompanied by his pounding for entry. "We're in trouble, *mon ami*. Serious trouble."

The door opened, the big Haitian entered. Cercueil stared into de Broglie's face. Louis was frightened, and not many things could evoke fear in the burly Ton Ton Macoute lieutenant. Cercueil felt a blood-chill crawl across his upper body. At that moment, he feared all his twisted dreams were about to come crashing down forever.

"Armed patrol boats, cruising along the brink of international waters!" de Broglie explained excitedly. "They contacted us by radio, warned us that they have orders to destroy the *Witchcraft* if we advance into Cayman waters."

Cercueil nodded grimly. "The Kingston authorities and those damn spies we met at the Palace of Madrid must have forced Griswald to talk or somehow found out the *Witchcraft* belongs to us."

"That's not everything we're up against, Pierre," de Broglie continued. "Another boat is closing in from the southeast, coming in fast. LeBou thinks it might be an old PT boat such as the Americans used during the Second World War. He says it's moving at approximately thirty knots."

"Coming from Jamaica," Cercueil stated. His mind was groping for some brilliant plan of action, but he found none.

"There's also a helicopter coming from the same direction," de Broglie added, tension straining his words. "I've told the crew to arm themselves and stand by for orders. Do we surrender or fight?"

"Maybe we can outrun them," Cercueil suggested.

"This boat won't go more than twenty knots," his lieutenant explained. "I'm in favor of fighting, but the ultimate choice is yours."

Cercueil opened the bottom drawer of his desk and removed a compact .380 caliber Ingram M-11 machine pistol. He shoved a 32-round magazine into the well and slapped back the charging handle. Cercueil held the M-11 in one fist and grabbed his swagger stick with the other.

"We fight," he declared.

**18**

The PT boat had formerly belonged to drug smugglers with South American connections. How they had gotten their hands on the vessel was unknown, but the smugglers had certainly taken good care of the fifty-year-old craft. Agents with the governor-general's security council had seized the boat less than a month before Phoenix Force had arrived in Jamaica. Colonel Wells had suggested the commando team might use the World War II battle-boat to pursue Cercueil's *Witchcraft*. Phoenix Force had eagerly agreed.

Calvin James, Rafael Encizo and Gary Manning stood on the deck of the sleek gray war vessel clad in black wetsuits, weight belts and rubber-soled shoes. They had Emerson air tanks, diving masks and flippers at the stern in case they needed to swim to the *Witchcraft*, although that would be done only as a last resort. The water of the Caribbean is too clear to provide concealment for swimmers unless they dive deep enough to use coral formation for cover.

Several long, gray shapes prowled the waters. The great predators of the sea also followed the *Witchcraft*: sharks are scavengers, and had been attracted by edible garbage tossed overboard by Cercueil's crew.

Encizo and James, experienced scuba divers, had encountered sharks many times in the past. They knew the big fish had a more wicked reputation than they deserved. Most species do not ordinarily attack human beings. However, some tiger sharks were among the sea hunters cruising the Caribbean that day. That was another reason the Phoenix Force trio did not intend to dive overboard unless it was absolutely necessary.

The PT boat was equipped with a .50-caliber machine gun mounted at the bow and a 75 mm M-20 recoilless rifle bolted to the deck on the starboard side. Encizo was stationed at the machine gun and Manning stood by the M-20. Calvin James leaned on the rail between them, an M-16 assault rifle strapped to his shoulder and a pair of Bushnell binoculars held to his eyes.

"They aren't running," James announced, watching the *Witchcraft* through the telescopic lens. "Guess they realize it wouldn't do them any good."

"Don't expect them to send up a white flag," Manning remarked dryly, kneeling by the recoilless rifle.

"And don't trust it if they do," Encizo added.

James examined the *Witchcraft*. It was a beautiful boat. The long white vessel resembled a giant ivory carving. Although equipped with an engine, the yacht had two masts with great blue-and-white sails stretched out to catch the wind. James was a Navy veteran, and once a sailor, always a sailor. The idea of making war on such a beautiful boat depressed him.

"Why couldn't those bastards have an old garbage scow?" James muttered sadly, aware they might be forced to destroy the yacht before the mission was over.

The helicopter hovered cautiously above the enemy vessel. An American-made Bell UH-1D, the chopper had also been supplied by Colonel Wells. The gunship was armed with two .30-caliber machine guns. David McCarter was at the controls. An experienced combat pilot, the British ace kept the chopper high enough to present a small target for the enemy, beyond the range of most small arms. McCarter handled the whirlybird with steady hands, although the fire in his belly signaled a battle was about to erupt. He could sense it the way animals can feel or hear the first tremors of an earthquake before the ground begins to shake.

Yakov Katzenelenbogen also sensed the approach of warfare. The veteran of a thousand battlefields, he knew the crystal waters below would soon be clouded with blood. He was positioned at the sliding doors of the flying gunship, strapped in place with a safety belt and armed with an Israeli Galil rifle.

He wished he was on the PT boat instead. Katz disliked flying, and he disliked flying in a helicopter more than any other method except possibly hang gliding—a sport he regarded as an aerial version of Russian roulette. However, Katz's prosthesis reduced his efficiency underwater. The men in the PT boat might be forced to dive, and the three Phoenix members on board were best qualified for the task.

"Oh, God," Katz whispered as he glanced down at the sharks swimming beneath the glassy surface of the Caribbean.

The Phoenix Force commander wore a life jacket, but he doubted it would do much good if the chopper went down in shark-infested waters. Katz's Jewish heritage had instilled in him a special fear of being devoured by the sea beasts. His desire to go whole to the grave had been crushed when he'd lost his arm in the Six-Day War, but he still hoped to be buried otherwise intact.

Katz switched on a battery-powered megaphone. His amplified voice boomed down from the Bell chopper like the voice of doomsday.

"Stop the engine and bring down the sails!" the voice demanded. "This is the end of the line, Cercueil! Order your men to step onto the deck and throw their weapons overboard! If you surrender now...."

Half a dozen crew members of the *Witchcraft* appeared on deck. All carried weapons, and not one of them intended to toss a single gun into the sea. Automatic rifles rose and fired desperate salvos at the gunship. McCarter swung the chopper away from the yacht, farther out of range of enemy fire.

"You stupid bastards," the Briton remarked as he gripped the firing mechanism for the .30-cals under the fuselage. "You don't know what you've started now."

Rafael Encizo launched the first Phoenix Force strike on the *Witchcraft*. While the gunship drew the enemy's attention, Encizo lined up the .50-caliber machine gun and opened fire. A chain of big cartridges rode through the breech as the machine gun roared. Large-caliber bullets smashed into the port side of the *Witchcraft*.

Railings splintered and chunks of wood spat from the cabin section. Glass shattered and bodies tumbled across the decks from the monstrous impact of the huge slugs. One slain Ton Ton Macoute hit man toppled over the rail. The fresh blood drew the sharks to the body. The fish seemed unconcerned by the battle above them as the wild feeding frenzy began.

Surviving members of Cercueil's crew ducked for cover and moved to starboard. McCarter brought the nose of the Bell chopper around, pointed it at the *Witchcraft* and brought it swooping down like a mechanical bird of prey. He triggered the two .30-caliber machine guns and bullets raked the starboard side.

The Briton saw two opponents convulse as slugs ripped into flesh and sent bodies twitching in a grotesque dance of death. The chopper passed over the yacht and rose into the sky before the stunned survivors could take aim at the retreating aircraft.

Encizo fired another volley of .50-caliber rounds at the *Witchcraft*. The captain of the PT boat, who had been handpicked by Colonel Wells, gradually guided his vessel closer to the enemy yacht. Wells had assured Phoenix Force the captain would not fold under pressure, and the PT boat commander was certainly living up to Wells's claims.

Bringing the gunship around for another attack, McCarter blasted the *Witchcraft* with twin machine-gun fire. The original six Ton Ton Macoute flunkies were already dead. The gunmen who took their places were also shredded by automatic fire. More bodies tumbled into the water for the sharks. Although their weapons were of no use against the war machines controlled by Phoenix Force, Cercueil's men continued to return fire with assault rifles and submachine guns.

Gary Manning held his fire in case the enemy had decided to surrender after the machine guns had raked their vessel. The tactic had not worked, so the Canadian launched the first round from the M-20 recoilless rifle. The big 75 mm projectile sailed across the water and smashed into the port side of the *Witchcraft*, near the stern. The explosive shell erupted with merciless fury. Almost a quarter of the yacht burst into flying kindling. Flames laced the deck while water rushed into the gap at the hull. The bow rose abruptly, and two more Haitian killers were thrown overboard into the terrible jaws of the feeding sharks.

The enemy vessel began to sink. Three surviving members of the crew discarded their weapons and grabbed the handrail. Terrified, they shook their heads to signal they no longer wanted to fight. No one else stirred on the decks of the doomed *Witchcraft*.

"Looks like they've had enough," James announced, scanning the crippled yacht with his binoculars. He recognized Louis de Broglie among the three survivors hanging on to the rail. The other two were not familiar; one was clad in a white lab smock. "I don't see Cercueil."

"Maybe he's already dead," Encizo commented as he unclipped a walkie-talkie from his belt. He pressed the transmit button. "Gray Eagle, do you read me?"

"Read you, Gray Thrasher," Katz replied.

"Enemy appears to be subdued," Encizo stated. "You see anything different from your position?"

"Just the three gents who look like they're ready to give up," Katz confirmed. "There could be opponents still inside the cabins."

"The boat is going down, Eagle," Encizo said. "If we want any of these hombres alive, I think we'd better get them now. Okay if I tell the captain to pull along portside and pick up the guys at the bow?"

"Watch out," the Phoenix commander advised. "These snakes might still have a trick or two left. We'll try to cover you from here."

"Okay," Encizo replied. He switched off the radio and relayed the instructions to the PT-boat commander.

THE *WITCHCRAFT* WAS nearly submerged by the time the PT boat eased along portside. Louis de Broglie, another Ton Ton Macoute enforcer and a terrified chemist stood ankle-deep in water. The bow was slowly sinking below the surface, and the frenzied activity of the feeding sharks had not ceased.

"Get your asses across the rail," Calvin James ordered, pointing his M-16 at the three Haitians. "Try anything and you're dead meat."

The starboard rail of the PT boat nearly touched the bow of the sinking yacht. Louis de Broglie extended an arm to grab the rail. His fist closed on the slick metal bar, and he hurled himself over the top to land on the deck of the PT boat near Gary Manning's position. The Canadian trained an FAL rifle on the Haitian. De Broglie stared up at Manning with surprise when he recognized the Phoenix warrior.

"You!" the Haitian exclaimed, hands raised to shoulder level. "You were at the Palace of Madrid...."

Manning rammed the muzzle of his rifle into de Broglie's abdomen, just above the groin. The Haitian folded with a gasp. Manning's right fist crashed into de Broglie's jaw and sent the man sprawling across the deck.

"I owed you that one," the Canadian announced.

The chemist jumped from the sinking boat and barely managed to grab the rail of the other vessel. Encizo gathered up a fistful of the chemist's smock and jammed the muzzle of his H&K pistol against his head as he pulled him over the rail.

"Lay down on the deck and keep your hands where I can see them," the Cuban instructed.

The second Ton Ton Macoute enforcer crossed over, and James promptly handcuffed him to the rail. Frisking him, he found a knife in the guy's boot and turned to toss it overboard.

Just then, Pierre Mazarin Cercueil aimed his M-11 at James's face. The Haitian master criminal had managed to swim from the flooded cabin of the *Witchcraft* and pull himself onto the handrail of the PT boat. His shirt and suit trousers were soaked, and water dripped from his face and hands. Although his eyes were filled with rage, a demented smile was fixed on his dark features.

James reacted faster than conscious thought. He hurled the boot knife at Cercueil's grinning face without taking time to aim. The blade sailed past the Haitian's right ear and landed harmlessly in the water below. The Phoenix pro simultaneously threw himself to the deck with the idea of bringing his M-16 around to point at Cercueil. But, he realized, he wouldn't be able to do this before the Ton Ton Macoute leader could pull the trigger of his Ingram.

Cercueil triggered his machine pistol, but it failed to fire. Water had clogged the mechanism and caused the Ingram to jam. James suddenly realized he was holding his breath, and exhaled. Cercueil tossed the weapon aside and vaulted over the rail. He had removed his shoes and socks, and his bare feet slapped the deck of the PT boat. James glimpsed the silver skull handle of the swagger stick in Cercueil's belt as the Haitian reached for the cane.

"Freeze!" James shouted, and aimed his M-16 at Cercueil's chest.

The thunder of rotor blades hammered down on them as McCarter swung the gunship over the vessels. The Briton saw Cercueil reach for a weapon, but he could not open fire with the .30-cals for fear of hitting his teammates. Katz leaned out the open door of the chopper, suddenly unconcerned about flying. The Israeli tried to train his Galil on Cercueil's back, but the movement of the copter made the task too difficult. If Katz missed, he might hit James instead.

Cercueil yanked the silver handle and drew a two-foot-long steel blade from the wooden sheath of his cane-sword. James fired his M-16. The automatic rifle spat flame, and three 5.56 mm rounds drilled through Cercueil's breastbone. The Haitian fell back against the handrail. He slowly glanced down at the crimson stain that covered his shirtfront. The cane-sword fell from his fingers.

"Wha—?" Cercueil began, the word choked off as blood rose into his throat and mouth.

"You lose, and it's time to pay," James told him as he stepped toward the Haitian. "We won and you're history, Jack."

James pivoted and launched a powerful high kick to Cercueil's face. The dying Haitian flipped backward over the handrail. Cercueil's bloodied form fell almost into the open jaws of an eight-foot tiger shark. The fish pulled the corpse deeper underwater, where other sharks joined in the meal.

"Hell," Manning rasped, looking away from the feeding sharks. "I don't think Cercueil has enough voodoo magic to come back after that."

James shrugged and tossed the sword overboard. "That's what I thought the first time I killed him," he commented as he picked up Cercueil's cane-sword. "But what Cercueil stands for seems to be prone to a kind of reincarnation, and I might have to confront this situation a third time one of these days ... but I'll worry about that when and if the time comes."

**A secret arms deal
with Iran ignites a powder keg,
and a most daring mission is
about to begin.**

# THE BARRABAS STRIKE

## JACK HILD

**Nile Barrabas and his soldiers undertake a hazardous assignment when a powerful top-secret weapon disappears and shows up in Iran.**

**The Badlands Just Got Worse . . .**

# JAMES AXLER

## Pony Soldiers

Ryan Cawdor and his band of postholocaust survivors make a
startling discovery when they come face-to-face with a spectre
from the past—either they have chron-jumped back to the
1800s or General Custer has been catapulted into the twenty-
second century. . . .

# TAKE 'EM NOW

## FOLDING SUNGLASSES
## FROM GOLD EAGLE

Mean up your act with these tough, street-smart shades. Practical, too, because they fold 3 times into a handy, zip-up polyurethane pouch that fits neatly into your pocket. Rugged metal frame. Scratch-resistant acrylic lenses. Best of all, they can be yours for only $6.99.

**MAIL YOUR ORDER TODAY.**

Send your name, address, and zip code, along with a check or money order for just $6.99 + .75¢ for postage and handling (for a total of $7.74) payable to Gold Eagle Reader Service. (New York and Iowa residents please add applicable sales tax.)

Remove from pouch...

unfold once...

unfold twice...

and they're ready to wear.

**Gold Eagle Reader Service**
901 Fuhrmann Blvd.
P.O. Box 1396
Buffalo, N.Y. 14240-1396

GES-1A

*Offer not available in Canada.*